THE DRESS

Natalie is a Bloomingdale's salesgirl, mooning over her lawyer ex-boyfriend. Felicia has been quietly in love with her happily-married boss for twenty years; now that he's a lonely widower, the time may just be right for her to make her move. Andrea is a private detective, specializing in gathering evidence on cheating husbands, and can't figure out why her intuition tells her the guy she's tailing is one of the good ones . . . Three people leading disparate existences — yet they have more in common than they realize. For their lives — and six more — are all linked together by one little black dress . . .

Jane L. Rosen is an author and contributor to *The Huffington Post*. In addition to writing, she has spent time in film, television, and event productions, and is the co-founder of the web- and app-based gifting company It's All Gravy. She lives in New York City and Fire Island with her husband and three daughters.

Twitter— @janelrosen1

JANE L. ROSEN

◆

THE DRESS

Complete and Unabridged

ULVERSCROFT
Leicester

First published in Great Britain in 2016 by
Century
London

First Large Print Edition
published 2017
by arrangement with
Arrow Books
Penguin Random House UK
London

A catalogue record for this book is available
from the British Library.

ISBN 978–1–4448–3410–9

Published by
F. A. Thorpe (Publishing)
Anstey, Leicestershire

Set by Words & Graphics Ltd.
Anstey, Leicestershire
Printed and bound in Great Britain by
T. J. International Ltd., Padstow, Cornwall

This book is printed on acid-free paper

Dedicated to the beautiful memory of
Ruthellen Levenbaum Holtz

'What is important in a dress
is the woman
who is wearing it.'
YVES SAINT LAURENT

Prologue

The Runway

By Sally Ann Fennely, Runway Model
Age: Just 18

'Pin it!' The dressers were all riled up.

Pin what? I thought. 'Ow!' There was my answer: pin me.

It was madness. I had been measured at least five times at casting. I thought that would be the worst part, fifty eager models lined up in black slips, dreaming of cheeseburgers. It was a different kind of cattle call from what I was used to back home in Alabama.

I barely uttered my first words of the day: 'It's big on me. Maybe you should put it on a bigger girl.'

'There are no bigger girls,' the pin-happy dresser mumbled.

I looked around. He was right. Last week I was skinny, the skinniest girl south of the Mason-Dixon Line. They called me String Bean Sally, asked if I had to dance around in the shower to get wet. Now I'm the big girl.

1

'Get in line!' he yelled. I got in line.

I concentrated on the mantra in my head: breathe, breathe, one foot, the other. Breathe. Breathe. The girl behind me broke my concentration with the strongest New Yawk accent I'd ever heard.

'I think you may have on *the dress*,' she said. It sounded more like a warning than a statement.

'The dress?' I didn't understand what she was talking about. I was having a hard time just breathing. We were getting closer to the runway.

'Every year there's one dress,' she explained. 'The front-row people out there, they choose it. See 'em?' She pointed to where two cavernous curtains met. As they rippled and settled I got a quick glimpse of the crowd. I wished I hadn't.

She continued, 'Come fall, those front-row people are gonna put that dress on the covers of magazines, on red carpets, and in store windows. And it's usually little and black, like yours.'

Her voice near 'bout erased her beauty. She was like one of those silent film stars my grandma used to go on about who went bust the day talkies came out. She sounded so foreign to me. I reckon if I spoke with my southern drawl she would feel the same way

2

about me. I'd hardly spoken since I'd been in New York for that very reason. When I do speak, it's real short and careful. I can fake my way through a sentence or two, but it's not easy. I try and triple my usual talking speed or people look like they want to wring the words out of me like I'm a wet rag. And my thinking has to keep up with my speaking, which ain't easy either. It's clear that they don't understand me just as much as I don't understand them. You would think that would make us all equal, but it doesn't. Not here.

It's not just talking the talk that throws me; walking the walk is equally hopeless. On my first day here I made the mistake of stopping mid-stride to look up at a building when *boom*, a man crashed right into me. He yelled, 'You crazy mama?' like I had slammed on my brakes dead in the middle of Interstate 10. I pictured the domino effect — a whole city toppling over on account of little old me.

The next day it rained. The city was hard enough to navigate dry, let alone in a downpour. I was so intimidated by the natives dodging puddles and raising and lowering their umbrellas in perfect synchronicity that I never made it past the overhang of my building. It was as if everyone but me had been taught the day's choreography in advance. I stayed put till the sun came out.

The girl with the voice was still going on about the dress. There were about a dozen girls between the runway and us.

'There was another possibility from a show yesterday that my friend Adeline wore. That may have been *the dress*. Adeline said the flashbulbs went crazy, especially when she was at the end of the runway. She's hoping it's hers. I want to be the kind of friend that hopes it's hers too. But I'm not. Honestly, I couldn't bear seeing her on the cover of *Women's Wear Daily*. *The dress* is always on the cover of *Women's Wear Daily*, right before it embarks on a sort of whirlwind tour of who wore what where. *The dress* can actually become famous, and its model too. I heard the girl from two years ago got a part in a Woody Allen movie. That girl was a brand-new face too, like you. You know, you only get to be a brand-new face once. They usually put *the dress* on either a brand-new face or a famous face. Now Woody Allen made her brand-new face famous! Do you think he's a pedophile? I don't like to think that.'

She didn't seem concerned at all with breathing, while that was all I could think about. Now there were just eight girls between the runway and us.

Still she kept going. 'Some things I wish I

4

didn't have to think about. Like last week someone told me those lemon wedges they put on your water glass are deadly. Covered in germs, even poop — that's what the girl said, on account of the waiters not washing their hands. Literally, that lemon wedge in my water is the closest I have gotten to a slice of cake in three years. Now what am I supposed to do? I wish I could unhear that thing about the lemons and Woody Allen.'

A *lemon*, I thought. All I had seen any of these girls have for dessert was a cigarette. They were all exactly the same — birds of a feather, we'd call 'em back home. They all walked the same, in a light, airy kind of way. I was sure they would flutter across the runway, while I imagined I would resemble a schoolgirl wearing mud kickers. And they all spoke the same language. They added words to their sentences that made no sense to me at all. Like *seriously* and *literally* and *honestly*. Honestly this and honestly that. It made you wonder if everything else that came out of their mouths was a lie. Also, many of their stories began with 'Don't judge me.' As if it were a get-out-of-jail-free card. 'Don't judge me, I slept with your boyfriend,' or 'Don't judge me, I ate an entire pecan pie last night.' Honestly, the second one would literally never happen.

Seriously, it's literally catching.

Six girls in front of me. I don't even know how I got here. Well, that's not really true. I got here on a Greyhound bus. When you're born with a face like mine and legs that keep going and going like mine, you stop considering any other way out. I used to do well in school, but there was almost no point. When my barely younger sister Carly and I would bring home our report cards, my mother would study hers and barely look at mine. My sister is short, like my mother's side of the family. An early bloomer, she was the tallest one in elementary school and the shortest by high school. She is okay smart, not a genius or anything. I'm just as smart as she is. But my mama barely looked at my report cards. 'With legs like that,' she'd say, 'you just need to find a rich man to wrap them around. Carly has to learn to fend for herself.' It was somewhere around then that I stopped trying.

It wasn't just my legs. I had the face, the skin, the hair, the whole package. That kind of beautiful that makes people stop and stare as if they're looking at a painting. A very tall painting. I was flawless. On the outside, that is. On the inside I was jealous of Carly. She would speak, and people would like her or not. Not me — I just needed to walk into a

6

room and the boys all liked me. Never heard a word I said. It was so lonely that I finally left and came to New York, where I could stand in a line of perfect specimens like me and be ordinary. That part had felt wonderful — until now. Just four girls ahead of me, all with the face, the skin, and the legs . . . Wait, three. I pressed my hands against my sides to stop them from shaking.

Her nasal voice briefly broke my nervous trance. 'It's not just lemons, you know. Those mints in the bowls at the register — those have been tested too, and . . . '

I hoped this wasn't *the dress*. It seemed so simple. I would think *the dress* would be something spectacular and loud, like the girl who was talking my ear off. The dress I was wearing was quiet. Not that I know diddly-squat about fashion. I know nothing more than what I've seen in the fashion magazines, and I only ever looked at those the few times that my mom drove Carly and me into Batesville to get mani-pedis. That's in fact how I ended up coming to New York. There was an article in one of the magazines — 'Do You Have What It Takes to Be a Runway Model?' I went down the list: Height, 5'9 to 5'11. Check. Bust 31–34". Check. Waist 22–24". Check. Hips 31–35". Check. They measured me right there at the salon. In the time it took for two coats of Cherry on Top nail polish to dry, my fate was sealed. There was enough money saved for only one of us to go to college anyway, and 'Carly had the brains.'

'Go!' With a push I was gone. It was like skydiving. Not that I know diddly-squat about skydiving either. As I stepped out onto the runway, bulbs flashed like mad, just like the girl had said they would. I near 'bout fainted right there. Honestly, literally, and seriously.

1

Seventh Avenue

By Morris Siegel, Garment Center
Pattern-Maker
Age: Nearly 90

As I rode the elevator to the sixteenth floor I
briefly allowed myself to dream about the
possibility of the cover of *Women's Wear
Daily*. We had made the cover a few times
over the years, but this was my very last
chance, the last fashion week before my
retirement. I had a good feeling about one of
the dresses. From the moment our designer
handed me the sketch I knew I had
something special to work with. Through the
heavy glass door I could see that the paper
had been shoved through our mail slot as on
any other morning. As I zeroed in on it I felt
my heart skip a beat. There it was! This year's
little black dress was mine. Worn perfectly by
some doe-eyed model who looked like it was
her very first trip down the runway. I made
that dress with my own two hands. The dress
of the season! It will arrive in stores around

August, a few months from now, and by the time its last reorder sells out it will be December and I will be celebrating my retirement. It feels good to be going out on top.

I am the first one in to the Max Hammer showroom every morning, at six a.m. Even today, as the last snow of the year dusts the Manhattan streets, I am still on time. On my time, that is. No one else will arrive for hours. I unlock the heavy glass door and pull it open, feeling victorious as I do. Pretty good for a ninety-year-old man. The words *Max Hammer Ltd.* are written in gold script across it. They have been there for seventy-five years. That is how long I have been pulling this door open, at first with the strength of a single index finger, now with two hands and a triumphant 'Oy!'

Max has been gone for eight years now. Before that he was the first one in. Sometimes I thought maybe he slept here. Not me: in at six, home at six. I never missed dinner with my wife, Mathilda, and our daughter, Sarah. She is in her sixties now, with two sons of her own. My younger grandson, Lucas, is an emergency room doctor; the older, Henry, plays cello for the New York Philharmonic. Max had two boys. The younger, Andrew, runs the business now, though in his fifties he's not exactly young, I guess. He is a smart boy, Andrew. Smart enough to know that unlike his parents, he has no eye for fashion. But he wanted into the family business anyway. So he went to Wharton and took over the day-to-day from his father when he and Dorothy finally retired around twenty years ago. Within a year of his arrival, Max Hammer went from being the knockoff king of Seventh Avenue to just the king, all without changing the name on the door. And I've been here, making the patterns, all along.

I met Max Hammer on the boat to America that left the Polish port of Gdynia in the summer of 1939. It was my older cousin Morris's ticket, and my father brought me with him to see Morris off. It was a week before my bar mitzvah, and I was sad that my cousin would miss it. When we picked him up that morning he was ill. Very ill, burning up with a fever. His mother, though worried, insisted he get on the boat to America. We looked alike, Morris and I. Though he was sixteen, he was small, and though I was nearly thirteen, I was big. People often mistook us for twins. His father had died years before, and he'd grown up with me almost as a brother. My father was a dressmaker and taught us both everything he knew, from how to make a pattern from a sketch to how to

11

make buttonholes without a machine.

When we arrived at the boat they would not let Morris on. By that point he had a rash covering half his body — you could almost see the heat coming off him. Now that I have seen nearly every childhood illness, I would guess it was roseola. The stewards turned him away, yelling that he would take down the whole ship.

My father took Morris's ticket, bag, and papers and led us around to the other gangplank. I assumed we were just trying a different entrance for Morris, but at the last minute my father gave me all the money in his pocket, all the money in Morris's pocket, and his gold wedding band. He kissed me on the head and told me to get on the ship. I cried, I begged, I pleaded. I tried warning him of the scene he would face at the house when he went home to my mother without her only son a week before his bar mitzvah. I looked down, embarrassed by my tears, and by the time I looked up he and my cousin were gone. I never saw my father or Morris again. Max Hammer, who was about six years older than I, witnessed the whole thing. He pulled me onto the boat by my sleeve and told me that my father had just saved my life.

It was three days before I could speak, and by then Max had told me his whole life story

— even the part that had not happened yet. The first thing he said he would do when we landed in America was find his girl, Dorothy, who had arrived months before, and ask her to wait for him. They had already been waiting quite a while. He said he had known she was the one from the first time she smiled at him through the window of his father's dress shop in Kraków. They were barely twelve years old at the time. He said that he would make the start of his fortune, then marry her and make the rest. Even in steerage on a rat-infested boat with barely a loaf of bread between us, I believed every word he said. He was larger than life.

I told him that I was to become a bar mitzvah on Saturday, and he arranged it that I did. I recited my Torah portion, and by the time we were halfway across the Atlantic the Germans had invaded Poland from nearly every direction. I endlessly worried about whether I would ever see my family or my homeland again. I went onto that boat a boy, but I landed in America a man. And not just because I was bar mitzvahed. I assumed my cousin's name, Morris Siegel, along with his age, nearly seventeen. I knew no one but Max Hammer, but I had a feeling that knowing him would be enough. Everything he had said would happen happened. Though not exactly in the order he predicted.

The very first thing we did was head to Brooklyn to find Dorothy. The photo she had sent was taken in front of a street sign at the crossroads of Coney Island Avenue and Avenue J. We waited all day in front of the sign. Max had shown me her photo so many times on the boat that I was the one who spotted her first. Their reunion was like nothing I had ever seen — I was too young to have had a girlfriend, and I couldn't imagine what it must be like to feel that way about a girl. The kissing and the tears. They both cried. I had never seen a man cry like that before. It wasn't just that tears filled his eyes, they ran down his cheeks relentlessly. Dorothy took us to a little dairy restaurant and we ate like we hadn't eaten in a month, which we barely had. I miss those dairy restaurants — they were once as prevalent as Starbucks in the old Jewish neighborhoods. Warm blintzes and cold waiters. Max told her of his plan to wait to get married until he'd gotten his business going. Then she told him of her plan — she didn't care that he hadn't any money, she wasn't letting him out of her sight again. They were married that week. She was really the boss, from the very beginning.

I was able to make contact with a distant

cousin in Jersey City who owned a dress factory, and I began to work there. As a pattern-maker's apprentice I fit perfectly into Max's grand plan, and I was happy to be working toward a rightful place in it. More than that too: the little we heard from home was not good, and doing the same work as my father helped me feel connected to him. The pattern-maker took me under his wing and I learned his way of making patterns, though I liked my father's way better. By the next year Max had convinced my cousin to back him in a dress house on Seventh Avenue. Besides lending him the money, my cousin lent him me, and in the blink of an eye the label Max Hammer was off and running.

The early days were my favorite. At that point I could make a pattern for any style. While the dress houses around us had fancy designers making original creations, Max had a different idea. He would send me to the newsstand every day to buy copies of Hollywood magazines: *Film*, *Photoplay*, and *Motion Picture*. If Carole Lombard, Joan Crawford, or Bette Davis was wearing it, we would knock it off. He had an incredible eye and could pick out just which dresses would look good on the average American woman while making her feel like a movie star. While most other pattern-makers needed the dress to produce a copy, I could usually do it from just the photo.

We weren't trying to fool anyone or anything. During Market Week, when the buyers came, we would leave the movie stars' pictures right out on the showroom tables. Our first line was even named for the actresses. Dorothy was a perfect sample size, and when she came out wearing the Greta Garbo or the Loretta Young, the buyers would break out the heavy pencils, as Max called it when they placed large orders. We were a big success, and by the next season other dress houses were copying our MO. But we were the first, and quite honestly the best. Before long Max moved his now pregnant bride from Coney Island to Central Park West. By that time neither of them looked like they had ever set foot in a Polish shtetl, let alone grown up in one. Dorothy now shopped at the finest stores on Fifth Avenue and the Ladies' Mile, where she bought the latest fashions from Paris and Milan. This meant I had more than photos to work from. I would take apart her beautiful dresses, study the handiwork, make a pattern, and put them back together. We were a dream team before the term even existed.

I found love as well. I fell in love with my Mathilda the minute I saw her on the L train headed home for Brooklyn. She was carrying fabric remnants that her boss had let her take home, and after sixteen stops I finally convinced her to let me carry them for her. She was almost a first-generation American; she'd been born on the boat — her parents had fled from Austria — and liked to say she was from nowhere and everywhere. Her parents welcomed me, and being part of a family again somewhat helped to ease my heartache. It was the summer of 1945 and the war had finally ended. People had brought back news of my family in bits and pieces over the years, and any hope I had of seeing them again slipped away with each horrific report. I knew that to honor them I had to live a full life, a life big enough for all of us. Soon Mathilda and I were married and had a child of our own.

There have been a lot of changes in the garment center over the years, but I have basically remained the same. Fashions come and go, but a pattern is a pattern. The shoulder pads of the forties and fifties were tossed out for the strapless numbers of the sixties and seventies. Unlike me, Max did change with the times. In the seventies he invested in discos, and he and Dorothy would dance their nights away. At least that's what I imagined — I never set foot in a disco. In the eighties they got into harness racing. They bought trotters and had their picture taken in the winner's box. They had a big life. Bigger than the shoulder pads that came back again in the eighties. I had a smaller life but wouldn't trade it for anything.

Eventually Max retired and he and Dorothy moved to Palm Beach. That's when his son Andrew took over the business. Max had lived the life he had mapped out on the boat for me all those years ago — his American dream. The only wrinkle was, he hated Palm Beach. Said everyone walked around in the same damn dress, the Lilly Pulitzer. He made his son promise never to knock it off. It wasn't worthy of a Hammer knockoff, he joked. But Andrew did not intend to knock off Lilly Pulitzer, or anyone else for that matter. Like his father, he too had a plan. His was to take Max Hammer to a whole new level by putting the craftsmanship and quality that we were known for into original designs. He went to FIT and RISD and interviewed designers and assembled his own dream team. They would hand me a sketch and I would create their vision. We worked well together, and I think it was the excitement of creating true fashion that kept me from retiring years ago.

The pattern-maker who comes in after me

will never make a pattern the way I do. I'm one of the last in the business to do things entirely by hand. I drape muslin on a mannequin and then draw the pattern onto cardboard. I take the designer's inspiration and make it come to life — my hands, my work. The patterns are all done on a computer these days. Some pattern-makers don't see an actual dress until a fitting. But whenever they do, one hopes they treat it with the respect it deserves. The right dress has a bit of magic in it. The right dressmaker is like the magician.

I imagine those shoulder pads from the eighties will come back again, but I will not be here to place them. This is my last fall line. I looked again at the photo of my dress on the cover of *WWD*. It has been a good ride.

2

The Movie Star

By Tab Hunter, Movie Star
Age: 29

I'm not really Tab Hunter, movie star. But today I may as well be. I'm really Jeremy Madison, movie star. Okay, I'm not really Jeremy Madison, movie star, either. I'm Stanley Trenton, nobody. My agent named me Jeremy Madison the day he signed me, six long years ago. But today, all day, he's been calling me Tab Hunter. As if being the subject of a false tabloid outing scandal weren't bad enough, he has to call me names. And I had to Google the name to even get the joke.

Tab Hunter was a closeted box-office star in the fifties whose agent created a phony relationship between him and Natalie Wood to cover up his homosexuality. I don't fully understand his reference, since the truth is I'm not gay and this publicity fiasco does not involve a bogus relationship. But according to the maniacal mind of my raving-lunatic agent, whom I'm secretly afraid I would be nothing without, the truth is irrelevant and I am the new Tab Hunter. I will give him this: like Tab Hunter's, my success is closely tied to my looks. I've made eight movies in the last six years, a track record that has brought me the overnight success and stardom that I always wished for. Careful what you wish for, I guess.

I wasn't a child actor, but close to it. I was cast in my first role just days after graduating from Los Angeles High School of the Arts. It turned out I'm quite castable. I'm the boy next door. I'm a high school rebel. I'm a geek. I can even put on a superhero costume and believably save the world from impending doom in the nick of time. I'm also turning thirty next year. So I am afraid. I worry that my days of playing twentysomethings are numbered and that there will be no place for me in the next Hollywood decade. It's partly because of this that I play the Hollywood publicity game as little as possible — it seems like the best approach to lasting fame. I avoid the paparazzi and a few years back even moved to Manhattan, where it's easier to keep a low profile. Being publicly outed, even falsely, was hardly keeping a low profile.

I was in a limo heading down Lexington Avenue to the premiere of my latest movie at the Ziegfeld. Hank, my agent, was screaming at me on the phone, making it very hard for me to think. Since his normal talking voice starts at the level of a scream, when he actually screams it's like he's screaming through a megaphone.

The fiasco that had him screaming began twenty-four hours ago, when I walked in on my fiancée having sex with her personal trainer. Apparently the trainer-trainee cheating scenario has become commonplace. The lethal mix of innocent touching and tweaking and body-clinging spandex often leads to much less innocent touching, tweaking, and body clinging. After the shock wore off I did what any actor in my shoes would do in that situation: I called my agent. Hank labeled the whole thing boring, adding to my mounting insecurity with this gem of a comment: 'The last thing I need is ten percent of boring.'

He claimed that as well as being boring, I would look bad if the truth came out. Can you believe that? *She's* unfaithful and *I'm* the one who'd look bad if the story were to break. He said it implies that I can't satisfy her. 'Sex symbols do not have fiancées who cheat with trainers.' He instructed me to keep the whole unfortunate occurrence among the four of us and attend my premiere tonight alone. When people ask where she is, as they will, because she is a Victoria's Secret model with celebrity of her own, I should 'just say she's under the weather instead of under the trainer.'

Truth? While it felt really crappy to walk in on that scene, part of me feels like I dodged a bullet. It was tough being with her. One star is hard enough to hide on the streets of New York — it's almost impossible for me to have dinner without interruption, or even see a movie. Try hiding a star plus a Victoria's Secret model. Especially one with no desire to be hidden. And two egos like ours would never have made for a happy family life. We both suck so much oxygen from a room that our children would've needed nebulizers just to breathe. Throw in my deep-seated trust issues, stemming from my parents' horrific marriage, and we were doomed from the start. I need a *nice* girl; a pretty girl, yes, but not one whose pretty is bankable. A girl I can trust with both my heart *and* my ego. And while my ego is bruised, I'm happy that it was bruised in private. So sure, it sucks to be cheated on, but now I'm free to find the right girl.

I felt like the worst was behind me. Until I woke up this morning and the worst was on the front page of the *New York Post*.

Jeremy Madison, GAY.

Seriously, that was the headline. I was enraged for so many reasons. First, over my complete lack of privacy. Second, that GAY is still news — front-page all-caps news, no less. Third, that it wasn't bad enough that she cheated on me and lied to me. To cover it up, she chose to lie to the whole world about me! Apparently she had no problem appearing barely clad on the pages of a magazine but wanted to appear saintly in her 'real' life.

Since no one told her I was going to remain silent — though Hank claims he told her agent, who promised to tell her manager, who was supposed to tell her publicist — she had obviously felt the need to get her story in the press first. The article went on to describe how she had been my supposed beard, covering for me to protect my multimillion-dollar career. (Enter Tab Hunter and Natalie Wood, once nicknamed Natalie Wood and Tab Wouldn't!) She cried about how difficult it was to be engaged to a closeted gay man. Night after night of rejection left her feeling ugly and empty, and she had to fill herself with . . . well, we all know what she filled herself with.

The reason my agent was just screaming at me is that I was refusing to take a shill to the premiere and refusing to make a statement. I don't think my sexual orientation or anyone's sexual orientation is news unless they want it to be.

I told my agent that I'm not interested in talking to the press.

His response: 'I'm glad that talking doesn't interest you, because if you don't talk now, pretty soon no one will want you to talk at all. At least not on screen opposite a leading lady for the ten mil you got for your last film!' He stopped screaming for a split second and said, relatively calmly, 'Did you wear the pink tie I sent over?'

I laughed. 'So we're embracing the gay angle now? You want me to wear a pink tie?'

'No!' he yelled. 'I mean yes. Yes, it's October first, breast cancer awareness month — I told you this, the whole cast is wearing them.' I had totally forgotten. He continued, 'Are you looking to give the press more evidence that you don't like breasts? You are to walk into that premiere with a woman on your arm and a pink tie around your neck or so help me god you will never work in this town or any other town again!' He hung up.

I looked out the window at the street sign — 63rd and Lexington, just a few blocks away from hundreds of ties. I alerted the driver. 'Sir, I need to stop at Bloomingdale's to pick up a pink tie.'

I entered the store at around six-thirty,

with only half an hour to go until the premiere. My plan was, I would walk down the red carpet at the last minute, alone, and avoid an inquisition from reporters. As I reached the tie counter my phone rang again. This time it was my publicist, Albert. He comes across much tougher on the phone than in person. Face-to-face he's a bit of a mush.

Our conversation unfolded like the setup for a meet-cute in an eighties romantic comedy script.

ME: Albert, what took you so long?
ALBERT: I spoke to Hank. I've been waiting for you to come to your senses.
ME: What senses? I stand at no comment.
ALBERT: No comment means you're gay.
ME: So? *You're* gay.
ALBERT: That's correct, but you're not. If you were, I would be your biggest cheerleader. But you're not.
ME: Did I ever tell you that my brother's gay?
ALBERT: The first day I met you.
ME: Oh, sorry about that. Well, anyway, how would it look to him if I made a big deal of denying that I was gay?
ALBERT: It would look like you're not gay.

ME: I think it would hurt his feelings.
ALBERT: You're being ridiculous, Stanley.

He always calls me Stanley when he is very serious about something. He thinks it grounds me. It doesn't.

ME: Don't you appreciate my attempt at solidarity?
ALBERT: What solidarity? You're not gay! Go solidate somewhere else and leave your brother and me be.
ME: I don't think *solidate* is a word. Hold on, I'm getting a pink tie.
ALBERT: A pink tie? Is that a joke? Are you trying to kill me?

I put the phone on the counter and asked the saleswoman, whose name tag read *Lillian*, for a pink tie. She was an older black woman with beautiful silver hair who looked eerily like my third-grade teacher, Mrs. Glass. It was clear that she had already recognized me and had been listening to every word of my conversation. She was slightly giddy, the way some people are when they see a famous person.

I had no idea what kind of fan she was: the kind who would keep her mouth shut, completely containing her excitement; the kind who would say, 'I hope you don't mind me saying, but I loved you in *Bridge and Tunnel*' (my last movie, in which I played a one-eyed serial killer, so it's odd for people to say they loved me in it). Maybe she was the kind who would ask for a selfie with me, which I doubted; there must be some kind of rule in the Bloomingdale's employee handbook against that. Or maybe she was the kind who mistakes her familiarity with me as one that goes both ways. This is more common than you might think. It's amazing how many fans will chat you up as if you know them as well as they think they know you.

Albert had not adhered to my request to hold on and was now shouting, a very non-Albert thing to do. He was so loud he might as well have been on speakerphone. The eighties rom-com continued.

ALBERT: Stanley, buy a masculine tie!

I laughed for the first time in two days. I picked up the phone for a second.

ME: I'm supposed to buy a pink tie. You and Hank really need to communicate better.
ALBERT: Please, Stanley, you need to

bring a girl. I will bring one for you.

ME: I don't mind you picking out my tie, but a girl? Forget it.

LILLIAN: I know the perfect girl for you.

Bingo. Lillian was the familiar kind. The kind who thinks my public and private personas are one. She thinks from watching me on *The Tonight Show* and reading about me in *People* magazine that she knows me well enough to fix me up. Albert heard her as well. He shouted.

ALBERT: Who's that?

ME: The lady who's selling me the tie.

I looked at her name tag again.

ME: Lillian.

ALBERT: Take the girl too, Stanley. Take the girl.

ME: Albert, this is nuts!

LILLIAN: What's nuts? She's a nice girl. Better than the big-mouthed tramp you were engaged to. I read the papers. Who's Albert, your agent?

ME: My publicist. She wasn't always a big-mouthed tramp.

LILLIAN: Not my business. Let me talk to him.

This couldn't get any more ridiculous, so I gave her the phone.

LILLIAN: Albert, let me bring him up to my friend Ruthie on three. She's like our resident consigliere. She can fix anything.

It had been a long twenty-four hours and somehow, after the betrayal and all the screaming, turning my life over to the Bloomingdale's mafiosi seemed like a reasonable course of action. Besides, I trusted them; unlike my publicist and agent, they were only making commission on the tie. Lillian, still talking to Albert on my phone, motioned for me to follow her up two escalator flights to the third floor. There she approached three other salespeople: a woman around her age who seemed to be the fixer, name tag *Ruthie*; a Latin-looking guy around my age, name tag *Tomás*; and a younger woman whose back was to me. At least she looked younger; I couldn't totally tell from behind.

They listened to Lillian intently, the consigliere eyeing me rather obviously, the younger one taking a quick peek over her shoulder, the guy staring openly. Her quick peek in my direction revealed that the younger woman was in fact younger. And she was pretty — unconventionally pretty and kind of sexy. I watched as she turned back to the group and emphatically shook her head: *No way*. She was refusing a date with a movie star. This just made her seem even sexier. But then Lillian whispered something in her ear. Whatever it was sealed the deal. She turned, walked over to me, and smiled. 'I'm Natalie.' (I tried not to dwell on the coincidence.) 'Give me ten minutes. I assume a little black dress is appropriate?' I smiled and nodded. She smiled back and was off.

Up close she was quite beautiful. Not model beautiful, thankfully. The kind of beautiful that radiates from her smile. The kind of beautiful I remembered from high school. Back then, before I was famous, I could trust that a smile was a smile with no further agenda. Now when a girl is nice to me, I have to question her motives. I hate being so distrusting, but fame has its downsides. Lillian handed me back the phone and I told Albert I had the date and the tie and that he should tell Hank I would be there soon. I promised to hold her hand, and when the press shouted questions at me I would just sweep by with my pretty date, saying that I was late.

'Just calmly late, though, not White Rabbit late,' he warned.

I promised to act calm and Albert was happy. Natalie returned in an elegant little black dress, and quite surprisingly, for the first time in a long time, I felt happy too.

3

The Red Carpet

By Natalie, the Beard
Age: 26

'That's a beautiful dress,' he said as we stepped into the limo. It was. I wanted to tell him all about it. How it was a Max Hammer, or rather *the* Max Hammer, the hottest dress of the season. How the first shipment sold out in just a week and how I was so excited to be wearing it, even though the price tag was digging into my back. But I didn't want to draw attention to the fact that I was only borrowing the dress and would be returning it after tonight. Not that borrowing it was such a terrible thing to do. I mean, I know it's not an excuse, but everyone does it. 'Buying' a dress, wearing it, then returning it is such a common practice that it was given a name — wardrobing. I guess once it was commonplace enough to get a name, retailers had to take measures; we got a memo just last week saying that giant tags are being created to attach to the front of all dresses, making them unwearable until the tag is removed. This little black dress that I'm borrowing may represent the end of an era.

'Thank you,' I said, like six beats later.

'Can I pay for it?' he asked sweetly. As much as I didn't want him to know I was going to return the dress, it seemed worse to let him think I'd bought a dress that cost two weeks' worth of my salary to go on a last-minute date with a movie star, so I came clean. 'Don't worry, I'm just borrowing it.'

He suddenly seemed embarrassed. 'I could have bought it for you. You could have kept it.' He added, a bit pathetically, 'You must think I'm such a loser, getting a date at Bloomingdale's.'

'No, I don't. I'm borrowing the dress, you're borrowing me.' I thought about what I'd just said; *borrowing* me made it sound like I was some kind of paid escort, but Lillian had promised me the guy was gay. She was tabloid-obsessed and whispered in my ear, 'It was all over the papers today. He's definitely gay, don't worry.' She knows me better than to think I would risk being taken advantage of by some scorned movie star. No way. And she knows that I have temporarily sworn off men, especially ones who walk into the store looking for a date.

'Please don't worry about it. I'm happy to

be going with you. I don't even want to keep the dress.' He didn't seem to believe me, so I changed the subject. 'I think it's ridiculous how much scrutiny you're all under.'

He nodded in agreement. I was surprised at how comfortable I felt with him. He didn't act like a big movie star. When I talked he looked at me — really looked at me, like I was the center of his attention.

'I hope you're not disappointed — the movie's not very good. And speaking of scrutiny, there's a chance that your face will be plastered all over the papers tomorrow. You realize that, right?'

'I never thought about it,' I lied. In fact I was counting on it. It was the reason I'd said yes without a second's hesitation once Lillian told me Jeremy was gay: the thought that maybe, just maybe, they would take our picture and put it on Page Six of the *New York Post* or, better yet, in that section of *New York* magazine that shows the most beautiful people wearing the most beautiful dresses in the most beautiful places. Either way it would stick it to Flip.

Flip was my ex-boyfriend. His real name is Philip Roberts. I couldn't believe he was ever my boyfriend, let alone now my ex-boyfriend. I didn't even want to go out with him at first. He had asked me out every day for nearly two weeks before I finally agreed. It was last winter, and on cold days he, like many commuting New Yorkers, cut through the store from Third to Lex, dodging the perfume sprayers, on his way to and from work. At the time I worked in men's gloves, where I would meet a lot of men, some of whom would ask me out. I heard it all. As Ruthie, my older coworker, would say, they were right off the cob. Lots of corny glove references like 'perfect fit' and 'looking for the match to this glove' and, the worst and most common, 'You know what they say — big hands, big . . . feet.' Which isn't even the correct reference, and is so not true, by the way.

Flip was less cornball than that. I didn't say yes the first few times he asked me out because he was older than me and short, with bad hair and a bit of a unibrow. But he grew on me. I didn't say yes the next few times because I liked it that the challenge was making him try harder. I didn't say yes the few times after that because it was beginning to feel like he wanted me just because he couldn't have me, like some kind of prize he was trying to win. My gut told me that in the end I might not be enough of a prize for him and I'd get hurt. This isn't about my insecurities, though I do have them — who doesn't? I'm pretty enough, and I'm smart and funny and kind, but he didn't really seem to value those things. He was a fancy lawyer who grew up on Sutton Place and went to an Ivy League school. I was a salesgirl at Bloomingdale's who had never lived outside Astoria, Queens. I had no desire to leave my comfort zone, and wanted to find a man who would love me for me. But he wasn't giving up.

Finally I gave in and we went out, and out, and out, for months and months and months, until one day, long after I had fixed his unibrow and fallen for him, he woke up and told me that something was missing. Something he couldn't put his finger on. More like something he couldn't put on my finger, as it turned out; two months later I read in the *Times* that he was engaged. Two months! The bride, I read, had also attended an Ivy League school and was also a fancy lawyer. They instantly fell in love at some fancy lawyer convention where they exchanged strategies, and no doubt bodily fluids. I bet it wouldn't have been so instant if I hadn't taken my tweezers to his eyebrows! After memorizing their wedding announcement, I continued torturing myself by writing *our* announcement in my head: *Philip Roberts to wed Natalie Canaras. The bridegroom is the son of Mr. and Mrs.*

Edward Roberts of Sutton Place and Sagaponack. Mr. Roberts attended Dartmouth as an undergraduate and got his law degree from Columbia. He was recently named partner at Hollingsworth, Hathaway, Horowitz, and Holtz, where his maternal grandfather, Frederick Hollingsworth, was a founding partner. The bride attended the school of hard knocks and is a salesgirl at Bloomingdale's, where her grandmother once successfully lifted a pair of size 6 black patent leather Chanel pumps. Ms. Canaras was recently named Employee of the Month.

I felt like a fool. He came into the store two weeks later. He was meeting her at the bridal registry. He couldn't have picked another store? He stood a bit too close to me while he spoke. As if he had a right to. The small talk was running out and I was beginning to feel vulnerable. I excused myself, saying I had to go back to work.

As I walked away he grabbed my arm. 'Maybe we can go to one of the dressing rooms and say a real goodbye,' he said, totally serious. I couldn't believe it. I had envied this Ivy League girl that he was marrying — now I just felt bad for her. Even with the satisfaction of knowing that he still wanted me, though, I was hurt, and months later I was still feeling vengeful. Tomás, my friend from the dress department, promised that after they registered we would totally get revenge by changing their china pattern every time someone checked something off so they would end up with mismatched place settings and multiple gravy boats. That seemed like fun and all, but my photo in the pages of the *New York Post* with Jeremy Madison was revenge on steroids! I was good enough for a movie star but not for Flip Roberts. For the rest of his life he'd be haunted by having let a good thing go. I would definitely win the breakup. It was perfect.

The movie star interrupted my thoughts. 'So, we should make a plan?'

I already had my plan, so I played flexible. 'As long as it involves popcorn I'm good. I haven't eaten all day.'

He looked worried. 'There aren't usually concessions at a premiere. I think they think it's tacky.' I felt as tacky as the MIA concession stand. He must have noticed, because he smiled his big movie-star smile and said, 'I think they should have popcorn too. I may even put it in my next contract!' He really was surprisingly sweet, this movie star. He continued, 'There's an after-party, but I don't think I'm up for it — too many reporters. Would it be okay with you if we walk the red carpet, take a few pictures, and sneak out for dinner before it's over?'

I was thrilled with this plan. 'Perfect!'

But apparently Jeremy Madison was less in control of his life than even he knew. His publicist, Albert, had told his agent, Hank, that Jeremy was bringing a salesgirl, me, from Bloomingdale's. Hank didn't feel the over-whelming confidence that Albert did in Lillian's matchmaking skills and panicked, leaking to the press that we were entering the theater through the back to avoid the red carpet. The press ran like cattle to the 55th Street door and the fans followed. We arrived to one newbie photographer from the AP who was too scared to leave his post on the red carpet. Unfortunately for everyone, he was so nervous that he shot on a used memory card and none of the pictures came out. His rookie mistake cost him his big shot at the front page and my big shot at sticking it to Flip. I guess people like me never get to make people like Flip Roberts feel less than.

Not yet knowing the unfortunate outcome of the photo, and with our stomachs rumbling, we snuck out midway through the movie. We got into the movie star's limo and the small talk that started with him asking, 'Where are you from?' ended with us in Queens, happily munching on tzatziki and spanikopita at my favorite Greek restaurant. It was the best date I had been on in ages, and somewhere between me telling him the big bad Flip story and him telling me about his parents' heartbreaking divorce and what it's really like to have no privacy, I began to wish that he wasn't gay. He walked me home and thanked me by joking, 'Bloomingdale's really does have fantastic customer service!' and kissing me sweetly on the top of my head.

The next morning I searched the Internet every which way possible but did not come up with a single red-carpet photo. All I found was a photo of us from behind on one site, Radar Online. It looked like nothing more than a cell-phone picture of us escaping out the back, holding hands like the good fake couple we were supposed to be. The headline read 'Gay or Straight?' and underneath, 'Who is Jeremy Madison's mystery girl?' I wanted to claim my place in celebrity history, to yell out, 'It's me, Natalie Canaras, third-floor dresses, Flip Roberts's old girlfriend!' But instead I got on the R train, little black dress in hand, and headed back to work. After all that talk about privacy, I would never betray Jeremy like that.

I walked into work to quite a reception. Ruthie and Tomás were eager to hear all about my night but equally eager to get their hands on the size small Max Hammer dress. Apparently it really is *the* dress of the season — this was the only one left in that size at any Bloomingdale's on the entire East Coast. The morning had been an eventful one, and my borrowed dress was at center stage. Ruthie told me the whole story.

4

An Age-Old Old Age Story

By Ruthie, Third Floor Ladies' Dresses Age:
A lady never tells

'ARTIE! Aaaaaaarrrrttttieeeeee!!!!' The screech-
ing was coming from the ladies' dressing
room. After twenty years at Bloomingdale's
I've seen nearly every kind of woman. But the
ones who shout out for their men like this
— usually some poor schlep standing around
holding her purse — those women are the
worst. It didn't help that it was Sunday
morning and I'd had one too many whiskey
sours last night. She sounded like nails on a
chalkboard.

They're a distinct breed, the men who
choose to wait around for their girls to decide
what to buy. It can take quite a while, as you
can imagine. It was much more common
when I started. *Taking the little woman to
Bloomingdale's to buy her fall wardrobe.*
These gals would actually go around the store
collecting their spoils, then hand them to the
men to pay. I always half expected Gloria

Steinem to come marching in yelling, 'Get a job, ladies, pay for your own threads!' That's how I felt, at least. I never wanted or needed a man to take care of me like that.

It's mostly the women who irritate me. I mean, first of all, what the hell are you screaming for? I'm right here. 'Excuse me, ma'am, can you please ask my husband to come look at this dress on me?' That's it — no need to scream like you're calling in two eggs over easy with a side of sausage at a truck-stop diner. And seriously, what is it that this husband is going to say anyway? 'That color looks putrid on you.' Nope. 'You are squeezed into that dress like a Polish sausage.' No way. 'You look beautiful.' Ding ding ding. That's your answer, and you might as well be asking Ray Charles. There are exceptions, of course. There's the cheapskate — he focuses on the price tag, making his judgment on that alone. I see this all the time. He rarely admits that his opinion is based on money, but once he sees the price it's 'I've seen you look better' or 'I don't like that at all.' Then there are the metrosexual/ sexually ambiguous fellas; they say something brilliant and tactful, like 'That neckline hits you in a funny place' or 'It would be nice to see more of your beautiful legs.' Smart men. Not as smart as the men who stay home, of course, but they have a clue.

Today, though, the schlep holding the purse was none of the above. His name was Arthur Winters, not AARRTTTIEEE, and he had been shopping with me since the old days, back when I started in accessories. He came in to buy a gift for his wife, not the trollop screaming at him from the dressing room. I remember it well. He was aces, Arthur Winters, the handsome, kindhearted type that still-single girls like me were holding out for. He introduced himself and said, 'I'm shopping for a gift for my wife's birthday. She always says she likes my gifts, and she always wears them, but I think she's just being kind. I want her to open every gift she ever gets from me with real joy, but I'm afraid I have little taste and less money.' Together we found the perfect gift. It was a black and brown hounds-tooth Oleg Cassini silk scarf. I said it was 'timeless and beautiful.' He said, 'Just like my Marilyn!' I gave him my card, and over the years, as his bank account grew and his browsing time dwindled, he began calling me on the phone to discuss his gift selection. Eventually his wife found my worn card in his wallet and came in. It didn't seem like she was checking me out in a crazy-jealous-wife way, more out of curiosity.

45

I was quite the looker back in the day. People compared me to Ava Gardner. Now that the in look is bordering on anorexic, the young me wouldn't have turned many heads, but back then women like me with full figures were in vogue. It was nice coming of age feeling good about my body and myself. It seems that the tide is changing lately for the better, with all these body-image campaigns and rounder young actresses proudly flaunting their stuff. I must say I'm happy about that. Breaks a saleswoman's heart to hear, 'Do I look fat in this?' all day long.

I remember that Arthur's wife bought a few things that day, and when she paid with her credit card I just came right out and asked her, 'Are you Arthur Winters's wife?'

She laughed. 'I am.' Embarrassed, she admitted that curiosity about me had gotten the better of her. I told her that I met a lot of husbands but few who spoke of their wives the way hers did.

We talked about her favorite past gifts, from the previous Valentine's Day's gray cashmere sweater, which she would love in another color for spring, to the patent leather clutch that she carried everywhere. She mentioned that Arthur's assistant had a birthday coming up.

'His other wife,' she called her with a smile.

'I always tell him to get her something nice. He does, doesn't he?'

★   ★   ★

I remember wondering if it was a trick, if she was testing me. Arthur did always make sure I picked out something nice for his assistant: two a year, one for her birthday and one for Christmas. I had met Felicia many times. He would often send her in to pick up Marilyn's gift. Pick up, not pick out. She was an attractive woman in a simple kind of way. But what really struck me about her was how kind she was. That and how much she obviously cared about her boss. The first time I said Arthur's name to her I noticed her eyes light up. I wondered if maybe there was something going on between them, but she spoke of his wife with such respect and admiration, and quite frankly, she didn't seem the type — and believe you me, I had seen the type over the years. In the end I decided, sadly and happily, depending on which way you looked at it, that Felicia was in a one-sided relationship with Arthur. And Arthur most definitely had no idea. He cared for Felicia very much, but as far as romantic love went, he had tunnel vision. His Marilyn was all there was. Until one day she wasn't.

Like the seasoned saleswoman that I am — third longest tenure in the store — I had Marilyn's birthday marked on my calendar, and last year it came and went with no call from Arthur, no visit from Felicia. At first I felt betrayed; maybe they had moved on to some younger salesgirl at the swankier Barneys or Bergdorf's. But I didn't think so. They all seemed so loyal. Finally I called Felicia at the office, pretending to be alerting her to an upcoming friends-and-family sale, and she told me the horrible news. Marilyn had been diagnosed with end-stage melanoma and had died only six weeks later. Arthur, she said, was devastated. I sent him a letter of condolence, and a few weeks later a box was hand-delivered to me at the store with the kindest note I have ever received from a customer. I read it so many times I know it by heart.

Dear Ruthie,
For the past twenty years of my life with Marilyn you were a part of every birthday, every Valentine's Day, and every anniversary. You helped me put so many smiles on her beautiful face. What I wouldn't give for just one more. Please accept this gift as a thank-you for all those smiles.
Respectfully,
Arthur Winters

I opened the box and there, folded neatly in tissue paper, was the brown and black houndstooth Oleg Cassini scarf.

★ ★ ★

'Arrrrrttttttiiee!'

Oh god. She was screaming for him again. I couldn't contain myself. 'What is it?' I asked rather curtly. I caught myself. 'Is there something I can get for you?' A muzzle, a horse tranquilizer?

'Yes. I need this in a smaller size. Do you see how it gapes here?' she said, pointing to nothing. She had on the Max Hammer dress we were having trouble keeping in stock, in a size medium.

'You do have to be able to breathe in it, honey,' I said.

She looked at me as if I was nuts. 'Just get me the smaller size, okay? And ask Artie to come in.' She was a nightmare.

I went to get 'Artie.' I thought I detected a bit of embarrassment in his face when I summoned him on her behalf. I could only watch them interact for a second before I had to turn away. How someone as wonderful as Arthur Winters could end up with a gold-digging twinkie like this was beyond me.

Tomás helped me look for a size small, and

while we looked I told him the whole sad story. He was particularly upset by it. Sweet Arthur losing his beautiful wife and ending up a stereotype. 'What about Felicia?' he asked. 'He should be with Felicia — she loves him!' I agreed, but what could I do?

Tomás, lost in his romantic idealism, suddenly snapped out of it. '*Dios mio!* We both know we don't have a size small in this dress — Natalie has the only one left. We have the one medium she has on and two larges.' I knew he was right but dreaded going back to tell her.

He must have seen it in my face. 'I'll tell her. Why don't you go out for a smoke?'

I hugged him. He was such a sweet boy.

As I put on my coat I could still hear her bitching from the dressing room. I peered around the partition and watched the scene play out.

'I need the small. Can you get one from another store? I *need* this dress. It's perfect. Artie, don't you think it's perfect?' He nodded, but she wasn't even looking at him.

'Can you please search for the dress and have it shipped to her if you find it?' he asked.

Tomás pitied him and knew Natalie would be bringing the small back soon. 'I will find one,' he said, 'even if I have to call the manufacturer. She will have it by tomorrow, latest. Will that work?'

Arthur looked relieved. 'Great. Please send it to her at this address. And it's my secretary's birthday too. How about one of those cashmere shawls on that mannequin? It can get a little chilly in the office.'

Tomás later told me that Arthur filled out two cards. One said:

A cashmere shawl to keep you warm! Happy Day!

He carefully put it in the little envelope and wrote *Felicia* neatly, in script.

And on the other . . .

The prettiest dress in town for the prettiest girl in town. Meet me at the Four Seasons, Tuesday at eight, to celebrate the big day!

Tomás couldn't help but ask. 'What are you celebrating?'

'Oh, our four-month anniversary. My girl-friend says in the first year of a relationship you celebrate each month. I'm kind of new at this,' he whispered. 'I'm a widower.'

I returned from my cigarette break right as the hussy hit the register with an armful of clothing.

'I'll just take these . . . I am devastated about that dress!' Devastated? About a dress? Really? There are people wearing recycled *I Rocked Becca's Bat-mitzvah* T-shirts in Africa!

Arthur smiled knowingly at Tomás, who smiled back as he rang up the staggering cost of 'just these.' As they left, the hussy thanked Arthur with a ridiculously wet kiss and a whiny 'Thank you, my handsome Artie.'

Within minutes of their departure Natalie arrived with the dress. Tomás's eyes lit up.

5

Eye of the Tiger

By Jeremy Madison, Movie Star

I woke up late, with a smile on my face, thinking about my night with Natalie. Since my good mood was unlikely to survive any form of social media or interactions of any kind, I decided to remain unplugged. Except for the delivery man from Three Guys, who brought me my usual Sunday morning double stack of banana-chocolate chip pancakes, I spoke to no one all day. There was a *Rocky* marathon on and I fell asleep somewhere after Adrian traded in her glasses for contacts. I woke up once to see Mickey die, at which I shed a perfunctory tear, and fell back asleep until the buzzer woke me. By this time Rocky and Apollo Creed were doing their ultra-eighties frolic through the waves. No one called *them* gay.

I hit the intercom and my doorman announced, 'A Hank and an Albert are here to see you.' I almost tossed my pancakes. Hank and Albert. Together. They never went anywhere together. I reluctantly told him to send them up and ran to my computer to Google myself to see what had sparked such a rare occurrence. By the time my doorbell rang I had pieced together the whole story.

They stormed in like gangbusters. Hank was on fire, as if he were on his ninth espresso, and Albert, poor Albert, looked like he had spent the entire day nibbling the tips off Xanax just to keep calm. I had seen him do that before. It's like he thinks it doesn't count if he just takes a little bite off the top, but eventually those little bites add up to god only knows how many pills. They handed me a printout of a TMZ.com story, as if they thought I didn't own a computer, and acted like my turning off my phone was a criminal offense. They were quite the combination, my agent and my publicist. When it came to me and my life, they usually had the instinct of a lioness protecting her cubs. Today they were like tigers on the hunt. Hank would shout out a solution and Albert would point out all that could go wrong with it. In the end, they agreed that the TMZ headline 'Gay or Straight? Who's Jeremy Madison's Mystery Girl?' was better for my career than just 'Gay!'

This bothered me for a few reasons: one, the paparazzi will now have even more reason to follow me to try and find out who the mystery girl is; two, I feel bad about my brother, I really do. He has been out and proud since we were kids and probably could care less about all this, but I feel as a good brother I should speak out against this kind of public outing of celebrities. And there was also a third reason: now it would be assumed that I was just a cheating louse who broke everyone's favorite Victoria's Secret model's heart. Truth? I really didn't want to be that guy.

But my advisers, whom, as I told you, I'm scared I would be nothing without, thought differently. Hank especially wanted no part of my gay-advocacy campaign.

He was adamant: 'Pick another cause, like the rain forest or puppy mills. And whatever you do, don't get caught kissing any dudes.'

They decided our best bet would be to answer the question 'Who's the mystery girl?' with a few staged red-carpet photos of Natalie and me, thus answering the gay-or-straight question as well. Of course this meant finding the girl again.

They were so anxious I thought they might explode — how would they convince her to go along with it, would they have to give her some kind of hush money, how would they make sure *that* never came out in the press, and on and on. The only thing worse than the two of them pacing back and forth across my living room would be the two of them detonated into little pieces and splattered all over my walls, so I gave in, agreed to their plan, and told them I thought the mystery girl would be more than willing to go along with the whole thing. They were so relieved they both hugged and kissed me.

'No kissing dudes!' I shouted, laughing, as I swatted them away.

I really agreed to do it for Natalie, so she could make Flip Roberts sorry. So that he could spend the rest of his life thinking about the girl that got away. I was sure he would, because I hadn't stopped thinking about her just from the one night. This plan also gave me a great excuse to see her again right away with no vulnerability on my end.

Albert snapped back into his usual state of despair. 'Wait. How do you know she'll do it?'

I alleviated their worry with one sentence. 'There's a guy she's trying to get back at.' Revenge — that they understood.

I put on the suit and pink tie that I'd worn the night before, and Hank and I headed to Bloomingdale's while Albert went to his office to arrange the photo shoot. Natalie had told me the night before that she was working today and I was excited to see her again, though I said nothing to Barnum and Bailey about it. God only knows what kind of media circus they would create with that information.

As we reached 59th Street I began to get nervous, and Hank must have noticed. 'What's up with you? You're doing that thing you do before a big scene where you chew on your lip.'

'No, I'm not.' I sounded like I was responding to my mother. I've been chewing on my lip like that when I'm nervous for as long as I can remember.

He dropped it and went back to his phone. I was nervous about seeing her again, nervous because I liked her. She was sweet, and had that I'm-not-going-to-eat-you-up-and-spit-you-out smile. Plus she was normal, so normal, which was refreshing. She didn't seem to care that I was famous. In fact, she spoke to me like I was one of her girlfriends or something. Suddenly it hit me. I hadn't had this experience with a woman in a very long time: she didn't like me. At least not in the way I liked her. This normal, pretty, sweet girl who acted like she didn't care that I was a handsome movie star *actually didn't care* that I was a handsome movie star. I would have to win her affections as Stanley Trenton. I felt anxious and awful. Maybe this was just some post-walking-in-on-your-fiancée-in-bed-with-her-trainer insecurity. Maybe I would realize that I didn't like this girl so much after all.

Hank shouted at me, 'What the hell, Jeremy, you're going to bite right through your lip! We're here, let's go.'

We got out of the car. I wished it were Albert with me so I could ask for a little nibble of a Xanax. Hank slapped a baseball hat on my head and pulled it down low as we headed up the escalator to the third floor. I wanted to say something cute to her and ran through funny lines in my head, but I had nothing. My insecurity grew, and I wished I had brought a screenwriter with me instead of an agent.

We approached, and as soon as she looked up and saw me I went with a quick-to-backfire joke. I held up a red dress and said, 'Do you have this in my size?'

She seemed not to get it and answered as if I was really asking. 'Um, I don't think that would fit you.'

'I was joking,' I said, somewhat defensively.

'Oh — sorry. I . . . didn't want to be politically incorrect.'

I didn't know what the hell she was talking about, but she followed it with her pretty smile so I chalked it up to awkward attempts at humor on both sides and moved on to explaining the situation. She agreed to the photo shoot, but there was one problem. Tomás, her associate, had just sent the very last Max Hammer small out for delivery to a customer. She called him over, and for some reason, which he refused to explain, he said he was almost certain the dress would be exchanged for a bigger size by Tuesday at the latest. Hank wasn't happy about the delay but texted Albert to set up the shoot for Wednesday. He told Natalie and me that under no circumstances were we to be seen together before then, and left mumbling something about his three wasted years at Harvard Law.

'I'm kind of disappointed,' I confessed to Natalie. 'I thought maybe we could've had dinner together again.'

She seemed thrilled by the invite. 'We can — let's go back to Queens! No one will be looking for you there. You could even hide out. I'm off work until Tuesday. We could be incognito till then — just in time to get the dress.'

Tuesday! I thought. *Maybe she does like me after all.*

I was in the suit for the photo shoot, so I went down to the men's department to buy something more casual for my furlough in Queens while Natalie finished up her shift. She said that she would meet me down there and we could blend right in with the crowd on the subway. I kept my baseball cap on the whole time, and there was something exciting and clandestine about the whole thing. Plus I hadn't been on the subway in such a long time, and never to Queens. When the tracks rose aboveground and I saw the outside world from the train, I felt like a kid. Natalie said I looked like one as well.

We walked the few blocks from the Ditmars Boulevard stop to her garden apartment. It was so nice to be away from Manhattan again. I imagined the paparazzi camped outside my building and loved the idea that they would be waiting for me all night. I didn't want to think about going home.

Her apartment was tiny and charming. Like her. One L-shaped room with a white fluffy bed filling the shorter arm and a long couch along the other. A big-screen TV hung in the corner, making it visible from either the bed or the couch. Natalie handed me the remote. 'Here,' she said, 'entertain yourself while I get ready.' The *Rocky* marathon was still on, and somewhere around the time Dolph Lundgren shot his first dose of steroids, Natalie changed out of her work shirt and into another right in front of me, as if I were her college roommate. The brief view of her sexy lace bra and belly-button ring threw me.

'What do you feel like eating?' she said. 'Let me give you the whole neighborhood rundown. We've got nearly every type of ethnic food you could ask for.'

'Surprise me,' I said, mostly because I hadn't heard a word she'd said. It's hard to get the full audio when the visual is so . . . distracting.

She seemed to love that answer and happily skipped to the bedroom, where I imagined her finding something to cover up her very sexy lace bra and her boy-pants underwear, which barely grazed the sweetest little belly button that I had ever seen. Never in my life had I met such a free spirit, and never in my famous life had I met someone so uninterested in me. This Flip Roberts must be something else.

She came out fully clothed, ran a wand of lip gloss across her lips, and clapped her hands together twice. 'Let's go!' I followed her like a puppy dog to a Moroccan restaurant where we sat on the floor and ate with our hands. She gushed, 'It's just like that scene in *Sabrina*, the new one, not the old

61

one with Humphrey Bogart and Audrey Hepburn, remember?' I didn't. She was surprised that I'd never seen either of them.

We talked about everything you can imagine, including how badly I didn't want the night to end. When I realized what I'd said, I bit my lip and added somewhat fraudulently, 'Because of the paparazzi at my apartment, of course!' She confirmed that I was genuinely invited to stay over.

When we got back to her apartment, she hunted through a collection of what looked like every romantic comedy ever made and found the original *Sabrina*. 'You have to start with this one,' she said gleefully, handing me the DVD. She dug through her T-shirt drawer and pulled out the biggest one she could find and tapped on her bed. 'This is my side. I'll just be a few minutes.' I got undressed and climbed under the covers wearing my boxers and a T-shirt that read *I don't sweat, I sparkle*. I tried not to let it add to my insecurity and waited to see whether she would reappear in sexy or BFF mode. She came out in sweats and a tank, plunked a big bowl of popcorn between us, climbed in, and turned on the TV.

'I haven't had a sleepover in ages. How fun is this?' she said.

This girl was definitely not attracted to me.

I couldn't take it anymore — I had to know more about this ex-boyfriend, who apparently so eclipsed me in every way that she was completely uninterested.

'Before we start the movie, I'm curious. Do you have a picture of Flip Roberts?'

She laughed. 'I burned them all!'

I looked at the cover of the DVD. Audrey Hepburn with a man on each arm: Humphrey Bogart on one, William Holden on the other. 'Okay, if one of these men was me and one was Flip, who would be who?'

'You'd be William Holden, of course! Humphrey Bogart is practically old enough to be her father in this movie, and he's not half as dreamy as William Holden.'

I looked at the picture again. 'Well, who does Sabrina choose?'

'You'll have to watch and see!'

I awoke the next morning knowing two things that I had not known the night before: first (spoiler alert), Sabrina/Audrey Hepburn chooses Linus/Humphrey Bogart, and second, that I could sleep with a girl without sleeping with a girl. I watched her sleeping for a minute as I consoled myself with the thought that she most definitely had daddy issues and I simply wasn't old enough for her. I lost myself in her simple beauty. Her parted lips and tousled hair. I wondered what sorts of things she dreamed about.

Eventually I snapped out of it and made enough noise for her to wake up, but not enough for her to know that I'd woken her. As soon as she was coherent I said, 'So, you spoke a lot over dinner about your mother, but I noticed that you never mentioned your father.'

'Good morning to you too!' She swung her legs out of bed. 'My father left when I was six. I was sitting in the living room playing Barbie dolls and he just walked out.' Now I felt bad for asking, though also relieved that I was right about the daddy issues.

'He just left? Just like that, no goodbye?'

She paused. 'Kind of. He said, 'Goodbye, sweet girl,' and I said, 'Where are you going, Daddy?' and he said, 'I have to see a man about a horse.' And then he left. That was the last time I saw him.'

She went about her morning business and I felt horrible. Here I was dragging up her emotional baggage just to satisfy my own stupid ego. I apologized as she plopped on the bed to put on her socks.

'I'm sorry, I shouldn't have gotten so personal about your dad.'

She laughed. 'My father lives a few blocks from here with my mother and has since the day I was born. You are so gullible!'

64

I pushed her onto the bed and we rolled around wrestling for a blissful moment or two. I wanted more than anything to kiss her, but the thought of her rejection kept me in check. She didn't have daddy issues. She just didn't find either Jeremy Madison or Stanley Trenton attractive. I decided I would meet her on Wednesday for the shoot and then never see her again. If I wanted this kind of rejection, I could go back to auditioning.

6

The Inception of
the Ostrich Detective Agency

By Andie Rand, Private Detective
Age: 39

As I hung up the phone after speaking with the woman who I was confident would become our one hundredth client, I couldn't help but smile to myself. Sure, things hadn't turned out exactly as planned, but they had turned out well. I was proud of the life I had created after my other life imploded, proud of the role model I'd become for the twins. A lot can change in three years.

It was three years ago to the day that I called an emergency meeting with my three best college friends at an out-of-the-way coffee shop just off the West Side Highway. When you admit to yourself that your storybook, love-at-first-sight, ten-year, honey-you-stay-home-with-the-kids-and-I'll-make-a-ton-of-money marriage has fallen apart, you don't want to discuss it at great length and varying volumes in your own 'hood. This felt particularly true when said 'hood was the Upper West Side of Manhattan, though my guess is that jilted ladies from Chappaqua to Chattanooga feel the same. Once out, a cat like infidelity is particularly impossible to get back in the bag. But holding it all inside was eating me alive, so I'd called my college roommates. We didn't see each other that often, but we found ways to stay connected. I knew they would travel to the ends of the earth for me, or, in this case, a diner on Eleventh Avenue that looked like it had been dropped there from suburbia circa 1969. It even has its own parking lot, which is unheard of in Manhattan, except for Tavern on the Green and a McDonald's somewhere in Hell's Kitchen.

Allison was the first to arrive but not to speak. At least not to me. She entered mid-call and unpacked the entire contents of her briefcase on the table. She was looking for a file and began handing me things one by one in a very chaotic process of elimination that I remembered well from college. The drill came right back to me, as I had spent hours and hours helping her tear through our room for a paper or her birth control pills or whatever it was that she was desperately searching for. She found the file she was

67

looking for and I recognized that calm smile of hers as relief. She spoke with authority.

'In the documents marked January eleventh it clearly states that Mr. Ackerman was out of town on that weekend.'

The person on the other end of the phone spoke, but Allison stopped listening. A large plushie plopped down in our booth, and both of us were momentarily distracted from our respective trains of thought — Allison from whatever case she was arguing, me from the end of my life as I knew it. If you had had a young child or grandchild in the past decade, you would immediately have recognized this plushie as Dora the Explorer. Knowing that didn't make it any less insane that a life-sized stuffed toy had squished its way into our narrow booth. Allison said, a little rudely, 'Excuse me, maybe you don't see well in that thing, but this booth is taken!'

Dora pulled off her stuffed head. 'Hola, ladies.'

It was CC, our other college roommate. Clearly I was not the only one with troubles.

'Gotta go,' Allison said into the phone, and hung up. 'What the hell, CC?' she shouted, as if Dora's presence alone weren't enough to draw attention our way.

CC shrugged. 'Brett's been out of work for

six months,' she said matter-of-factly. 'I needed a job.'

'You graduated magna cum laude from Wesleyan, for god's sake — this was all you were qualified for?' Allison was still in outraged-lawyer mode.

I came to CC's defense. 'She *was* a Spanish major.' Allison didn't have children; she stared at me blankly. 'Dora's Spanish.' I smiled.

'It did help me get the job,' CC happily chimed in. She looked at Allison's disappointed face. 'Come on, Allison. What do you think my résumé looks like at this point? It was basically this or sex worker.'

Allison wasn't having it. 'That's BS. You can do anything.'

CC's problems simultaneously made me feel better and further scared the crap out of me. I thought about my dilemma while Allison continued her interrogation. I knew it was only a matter of minutes before CC would no longer be able to take it and would turn the conversation toward me. After all, I was the one who'd called the emergency session.

I looked over at CC, her Dora backpack squeezed up against the rim of the table, and decided to spare her further misery and just come out with it. 'Derek is cheating on me,'

69

I said, stopping them dead in their tracks. I love it when people act just as you expect them to. I pulled out a folder; I had compiled a treasure trove of damning facts, incriminating photographs, and logically drawn postulations. I'm not one to fall quickly into paranoia or victimization, and Allison and CC know that about me. So they knew this was serious.

I'm a good judge of character, and when my gut tells me something, it's usually correct. There were not a million signs of infidelity, like people say to look for. 'Is your spouse wearing new aftershave?' He wasn't. 'Is your spouse suddenly working out more, concerned with his appearance?' Derek was always vain and in good shape. There was just this one thing that was bothering me. I told them the whole story.

For years we had fought the same way, and suddenly he was fighting differently. Like intentionally picking a fight and then storming out to 'cool off.' After it happened a few times I thought maybe he'd started smoking again. We'd made a pact to quit together a few years earlier, and I thought maybe this was what he was hiding. I started smelling him when he came back, and at first I thought I was right. He wouldn't smell like cigarettes, but he always smelled so clean.

Like someone covering it up with soap and toothpaste. It went on for months, and I just never confronted him. I thought there were worse things than smoking and covering it up. Like cheating, for example. Then one day he picked a fight with me over a game of Words with Friends. I put down the word *muzjiks* on a double word score, using all seven letters for, like, 147 points, and he was like, what does *muzjiks* even mean? And I kind of knew what it meant but didn't feel like defending myself, so I just said I didn't remember. He accused me of cheating. Said there was something called Words with Friends Cheat and that I was a cheater. He stormed out, without a coat, which I noted because it was raining. I went over to his computer and clicked history and there it was — Words with Friends Cheat. *He* was the cheater. I said it out loud to myself right there alone in our apartment: 'He's the cheater.'

'Oh my god, Andie, seriously?' Allison interrupted me, laughing. 'You had us worried.'

CC was annoyed. 'I ditched a book fair in Tribeca to come here, and he was cheating at Words with Friends?'

Looking at CC, Allison again shook her head in disappointment. CC attempted to defend herself. 'Swiper and Diego will have to cover for me all day.'

'Let me finish!' I protested. 'All I'm saying is that before that point, it never entered my mind that he would cheat. But the minute I saw the word *cheat* a lightbulb went off in my head. I jumped in the elevator and went to the lobby, hoping with all my being to see him smoking with Miguel the doorman. Miguel was outside smoking, but he was alone. So I asked him, 'Miguel, which way did Mr. Banks go when he left?'

'Miguel was nervous, said he hadn't seen him. But I pleaded with him. I told him I wasn't mad at all, I totally knew what Mr. Banks had been up to, and I really didn't care that he was covering for him. He panicked and started blabbering about how maybe I wouldn't be mad but Mr. Prescott would be furious, and he hadn't wanted to be their lookout, he didn't want to lose his job, but at that point I stopped hearing what he was saying because I had put it together: Derek's been having an affair with Chelsea Prescott from the sixth floor of our building. Every time Rick Prescott leaves to ride his bike around the outer loop in Central Park, my husband's riding his wife around their bedroom.'

I pointed to Exhibit D in my folder, a picture of Derek getting off the elevator on the sixth floor. 'Miguel is on my payroll now,' I said. 'So I have the elevator pictures to prove it.'

CC was silent.

Allison was outraged. 'Did you confront him?'

'No. Not yet. I started looking for evidence everywhere — from the trash in our bedroom to the trash on his computer. Then I put a GPS in his briefcase; he arrives at our building sometimes an hour before he comes home and sometimes in the middle of the day. I installed an app on his phone that lets me see who he's called.' I showed them the printout. 'Here, see? The highlighted phone numbers are her cell.' Allison's mouth was wide open. I was surprised. 'I can't believe you're so shocked — you must see this kind of thing with clients all the time.'

'I'm shocked by the case you've built against him. You did all this on your own?'

I nodded my head, feeling good about myself for the first time in a long time.

'You know, most women just stick their heads in the sand,' she said, full of admiration. 'You're really going to be able to screw him in the divorce!' Hearing that word out loud made it seem inevitable. Oddly, I started laughing uncontrollably. Soon all three of us were laughing, though none of us really knew what was funny.

Allison was the first to regain control. She turned to CC. 'CC, what's a muzjik?'

CC laughed. 'It's a Russian peasant.'

Allison shook her head. 'No more Dora the freakin' Explorer, CC. You are two of the smartest women I know.'

We stopped laughing. She was right.

That was the day the idea for the Ostrich Detective Agency was born. CC and I got our PI licenses. Allison fed us our first clients, and word of mouth got us the rest. Three years later and here I was, talking to our hundredth client. Her name was Caroline Westmont and she reminded me a lot of myself. I was looking forward to meeting her.

7

Guess Who's Coming to Dinner?

By Tomás, Third Floor Ladies' Dresses
Age: 27

It had been a couple of days, and I was starting to get nervous about what I'd done with the dress. I don't know why I always have to be such a *metiche* — translation, buttinski. They even created a category just for me in my high school yearbook: Most Likely to Butt In. As I carried that last size small Max Hammer over to gift wrap like a lamb to slaughter, I realized that it was doubtful we would receive another shipment. I loved this dress. It was one of those head-turners that make every girl feel like the belle of the ball. I couldn't bear for that ungrateful child to get such a treasure — the dress or Arthur Winters. So I butted in! I sent the last size small little black dress with the invitation for dinner to Arthur's age-appropriate secretary and the matronly cashmere throw to the gold digger! I thought about all the possible repercussions. The worst-case scenario was that I would get fired for messing up an order. I doubted that, though. Charlene from lingerie was still boasting about the time she purposely sent a lace teddy to a lecherous customer's wife instead of his girlfriend. That card read 'Just 24 hours till she leaves to visit her mother!' This was tame compared to that.

The second-worst-case scenario was that Arthur's adoring secretary would get her hopes up at being invited for dinner and arrive to see Artie's face fall in disappointment. This scenario made me ill. The thought of sweet, caring Felicia all excited to finally be noticed and Artie still being too lost in grief to recognize true love was right out of one of my *abuela's* *telenovelas*. *Dios mio!* What had I done?

'Excuse me, I would like to exchange this dress for a bigger size.' And there she was, right in front of me, dress in hand. By the grace of god I didn't throw my arms around her and yell out 'Felicia!' I had bet on the likelihood that middle-aged Felicia wouldn't be the same size as the Skinny Minnie harlot, and I'd been right! Thank god she'd thought to try the thing on in advance. But of course she had; she'd been waiting for this date for seventeen years.

'Can you help me?' she added, with not a hint of annoyance at my being lost in my own romantic daydreams.

I snapped to attention. 'I am so sorry, lost in thought, yes, I can absolutely help you with that.'

I set her up in a dressing room, and when I knocked to see if she needed anything, she asked my opinion on the fit.

'It's perfect!' I said, meaning it.

'It is!' she responded joyfully. She spun around like a schoolgirl. 'This may be the most beautiful dress I've ever worn.'

Then out came the buttinski. 'What shoes are you going to wear with it?' She pointed to the at-*least*-two-seasons-ago black pumps on her feet. No good. 'We're having a secret sale today,' I lied; I'd give her my employee discount. 'If you want, we can lock this door with your stuff inside and go to the shoe department together!'

'Okay, thanks!' She beamed. 'This is a special night.'

'Really?' I replied, as if I didn't know. 'You can tell me all about it on the way there.'

We headed to the second-floor shoe department and picked out a pair of sexy black suede sandals with a heel. It took me forever to steer her away from the practical pumps that she was used to.

'You have the best taste, Tomás. Thank you so much.'

'That's what happens when you spend half your life in a closet.'

She laughed. Sitting on the soft couches in the shoe department, she opened up to me about Arthur and her unrequited love for him. She told me how it broke her heart to see him in such pain after his wife died and how her friends at work said that she should make her move. Unknown to her, they had all been aware for years that she was in love with him. Everyone could tell. Everyone except Arthur. She waited what she thought was the appropriate amount of time, six months, but still she couldn't get up the nerve. Then one day Arthur's oldest daughter, Jessica, called and asked if she would join them for a Labor Day weekend barbecue. The invitation had felt like the daughter's blessing. Felicia was thrilled and baked a perfect seven-layer cake. It took three tries, but she did it; she took the other, almost-perfect fourteen layers to the soup kitchen where she volunteers. This woman is a total gem.

We bought the shoes, and I convinced her to let me take her to the first floor for a makeover. By now I could have convinced her to get an *I* ♥ *Artie* tramp stamp. At the makeup counter, in between pursing her lips and widening her eyes, she finished the story of the Labor Day debacle. She walked in, cake in hand, and was greeted very warmly by Arthur's daughter. She thanked her for the cake and took her aside.

'Felicia, I know my dad is devastated by my mother's death and it will take him a while to come out of that. In the last weeks of her life my mother confided in me that her greatest fear wasn't dying. It was that my father would be alone. She asked that I guide him toward a wonderful woman. She specifically said, 'Someone like Felicia.'' Felicia had been so taken aback that tears had formed in her eyes. As she blinked them away, Arthur walked in with a scantily clad and overly perfumed young lady, who he introduced as Sherri. (Only a gem would describe that harlot as a young lady.) 'My heart broke,' she said. 'My hands began to shake and I had to give the cake to Jessica, as it was now shaking too.' Jessica was utterly gracious — she had learned from the best. She welcomed Sherri and introduced her to Felicia. When Arthur and Sherri were out of earshot she whispered, 'I'm so sorry, Felicia, I had no idea.' Felicia smiled and assured her that she was okay. But of course she wasn't.

So tonight, Arthur inviting her for dinner at the Four Seasons — well, this was the most promising thing to happen to her in like . . . ever. The makeup artist turned Felicia toward him to concentrate. As I watched her take herself in in the mirror, my mind was beginning to fill with dread, thinking of the possibility of her evening ending poorly. I vowed never to butt into other people's business again. My thoughts wandered to what God and Ruthie would have in store for me as a punishment when 'Voilà!' The makeup artist spun Felicia around. She looked beautiful. All my worries melted away. If Arthur Winters could not see the jewel in front of him, so be it. It was time for Felicia to move in or move on. I told her exactly that, and she left Bloomingdale's with renewed confidence.

There's a good chance I'll never know what happens tonight. That's one of the more unfulfilling parts in the life of a salesperson. Everyone comes in searching for the perfect dress for her big day, whether it's her high school prom or her fiftieth high school reunion. The dress needs to match more than just the shoes. It needs to match her hopes and expectations. It needs to remove all worry and doubt about looking good from the equation so that everything else can fall into place. While I'm 100 percent in on the groundwork, I rarely get to hear the outcome.

This time I was overly invested and would be thinking about Felicia long after she left the store.

As promised, I hid the size small Max Hammer she had returned in the back room for Natalie to wear to her photo shoot with the movie star. I also promised her that I would not hit on him if he ever comes into the store again. In return she promised that when he officially comes out she'll fix us up!

8

The Hundredth Client
of the Ostrich Detective Agency

By Andie Rand, Private Detective

Caroline Westmont entered my office at three o'clock sharp, dressed impeccably in Chanel from sunglasses to shoes. She looked completely together until she lowered her shades to reveal puffy, tear-stained eyes. I remembered those days of constant crying. Having to hide it from my children, as she may be trying to hide it from hers. My poor dog, Franny, saw a lot of tears that first year. I was sometimes surprised that she didn't take a piece out of Derek when she saw him. Aside from suggesting that they get a dog, I always wanted to tell clients, 'You'll be fine. Look at me — I was once where you are and I'm doing great!' But that's not my place. I'm not a shrink, and in this job I learned quickly that similar situations often yield different outcomes. Not everyone feels the same way about infidelity that I did. For me there was no turning back. But there are many couples who come out the other end and stay till death do them part — that death, hopefully, not by the hand of the scorned spouse.

As always, I asked for the entire story of John and Caroline Westmont. She relayed the brutal tale in its entirety, and as usual in cases like this, it struck a chord. They always did when it came to one spouse cheating on another. It was hard work for me not always to assume the worst, especially when it comes to men. I don't want to become one of those bitter, untrusting women. And as a professional I certainly don't want to come across that way. I work hard to keep an open mind and to pass judgment only on evidence and facts. But in this case the facts were simple.

Caroline was positive that her husband was cheating on her with his masseuse but had no evidence to back it up. When they had married, nearly twelve years earlier, she had signed an ironclad prenuptial agreement with only one stipulation: if either party cheated, the prenup became invalid. At the time she had been insulted that his family was making her sign a prenup, and they had fought about it a lot. John came from a very wealthy, old-money family that was dead set on it. After much back-and-forth, one compromise was agreed upon: the infidelity clause. They agreed that if John were to have an extramarital affair, he would have to pay Caroline an additional $5 million in the divorce. She signed the papers a week before the wedding.

It was a beautiful wedding at the Cathedral of St. John the Divine and the newlyweds moved into an apartment just down the block on 116th Street. It was small compared to the sixteen-room apartment on Fifth Avenue where John had grown up, but it was close to his job, and they felt very bohemian. As she told the story I wondered what had caused her transformation, as *bohemian* was the last word I would use to describe her.

John was a professor of film at Columbia University. About five years into the marriage, when their daughter Chloë was two, John's parents died together in a horrible car accident on the Amalfi Coast. (If you've ever driven on that road, you have most likely pictured a similar fate befalling you.) When the dust settled, John, Caroline, and Chloë moved into his parents' Fifth Avenue apartment. From then on things quickly changed. The money had always been there, but they had never needed or spent it; now it infiltrated their lives. John's parents' staff waited like puppies at a pound to see if they were to keep their jobs. Of course they kept them; John and Caroline felt it was their duty.

The moldings needed dusting and the twenty-four-seat dining room table screamed out to be set and sat at. 'So,' Caroline said, 'I rose to the occasion. At first it was a big adjustment for me to be that social. John is really the more social of the two of us. But I loved John, and I did my best to embrace my new role.'

Fast-forward through seven years of smiling while hosting cocktail parties for the parents of Chloë's classmates at Spence, faculty dinners for John's Columbia colleagues, and luncheons for the Junior League, and Caroline seemed happy and settled in her inherited role. Until the day when a hard-bodied masseuse named Anna entered the picture and misaligned the stars.

I had to interrupt. 'Hold on, Caroline — you're telling me John is a professor at Columbia and you think he's been faithful all this time? I mean, coeds and professors — it's a cliché for a reason.'

She thought about it before responding. 'That's too obvious for John. He likes to come across as so good. He wouldn't want anyone to think otherwise, especially at Columbia.'

'He sounds like a hypocrite,' I said.

She smiled. 'Exactly.' She hugged me when she left and said warmly, 'At first I thought I would just leave him — the money really doesn't mean all that much to me. But then I thought, *He should pay.*'

We agreed that she would give me access to their apartment and his schedule and we would speak as soon as I had something. Luckily, she had just purchased new cell phones, with her name on all three contracts, so tracking them was her right. I was confident that with all those resources it wouldn't take long for me to expose John for the degenerate that he was.

9

Dinner at the Four Seasons

By Felicia (aka Arthur Winters'
Executive Assistant)
Age: 52

The Four Seasons is one of those celebrated restaurants in Manhattan that rises to the status of cultural icon. As revered as beloved New Yorkers like Walt Frazier and Fiorello La Guardia, and hailed alongside establishments from the Rainbow Room to the Carnegie Deli. Like the chicken and the egg, it's hard to determine whether New York created these legends or these are the legends that created New York.

I had never stepped inside the Four Seasons before. Well, that's not entirely true. Long ago I stepped into the coatroom, where a hatcheck girl assured me she would get a forgotten file to my boss, Mr. Winters, who was there having a power lunch. I believe the term *power lunch* was actually coined at the Four Seasons. Sadly, there's talk that it may be closing, losing its lease. If that happens, I imagine Fortune 500 execs will be wandering the streets in search of the new place to see and be seen. Seems that someone should stand up and fight for such a legend.

Back then I still called him Mr. Winters. It wasn't long after that power lunch before I started calling him Arthur. Not much longer than that before I had fallen in love with him. Tonight we would be dining at the Four Seasons together, I hoped in the famed Pool Room. But it didn't really matter to me very much where we dined. I was going on a date with Arthur Winters, the man I had loved for seventeen years. I honestly never thought this day would come. I looked at my watch. I was five minutes early. That wouldn't do. I headed inside to the ladies' room to check my face in the mirror.

Though this was my first date with Arthur Winters, in truth I had been having an affair with him for seventeen years. Unlike other, more torrid affairs, when the wife has no clue, in this case the husband himself had no clue. I sometimes think that maybe Marilyn did know that I was in love with her husband. I was pretty sure half the office knew. But Arthur? Arthur had no idea. When it came to love, he had tunnel vision. His wife and daughters were everything to him. Marilyn was very confident about their bond and never treated me with anything but gratitude for looking after the man she loved from nine to five, Monday through Friday. Arthur simply loved his wife and didn't have eyes for anyone else. It was one of the things I loved about him. In all the time that I've worked for him I've never made an inappropriate move.

I don't want you to think I'm pathetic. I haven't remained stagnant on the dating front. At times I've dated a lot, attending singles functions and putting it out there to friends that I would like to be fixed up. At other times I've become tired of it and been content just to hang out with girlfriends and join movie and theater clubs and whatnot. But I did try to find a man of my own. When your heart is already spoken for, though, it's hard to give it to someone else. I would have had to be knocked over the head with a bat to see past Arthur, and truth be told, no one came out swinging.

Even on the handful of occasions that I had sex over the years, I pictured Arthur the entire time. When the man my cousin Stacey had fixed me up with came up to my apartment after a few too many margaritas at Rosa Mexicano, it was Arthur's hand that gently unzipped my dress and caressed my back. It was Arthur who was the real object of every moment of desire I have had over the past seventeen years. Not once did I open my eyes to look at who I was actually with. Not once did I picture anyone else. At this point I think if I were ever to be alone with him, one real-life touch from him in the right place and I might just explode right there on the spot!

You may think I'm crazy, but I believe you can't help who you fall in love with. Maybe you're in love with the correct person, the one who's right around your age, your same religion, someone your parents were thrilled to meet when you took him or her home. If you are, well, then you probably don't believe me. But you might just as easily have fallen for your lab partner in college, who came to your northeastern liberal arts school from some rural town in the Appalachians, and the minute her hand brushed against yours while reaching for a beaker you knew you were a goner. And you wouldn't have cared if she was a he or he was a she or if he or she was already with someone else. That's what happened to my freshman roommate in college. There she was, dating the star of the football team, when some girl from Kentucky came in and made off with her heart. Done. You can't help who you fall in love with. That kind of love just swoops in and grabs hold of you, and even if you were to drop chemistry — or switch jobs, which god knows I should have done a long time ago — it's still taken hold of your desire, and that's a damn hard thing to free yourself of.

I am in love with Arthur Winters and have been for a very long time. And until yesterday, when I received this beautiful dress and an invitation to the Four Seasons for dinner, I never thought it possible that the feeling could ever become mutual. I can't lose sight of the fact that it's only possible because a beautiful woman is no longer with us. But I'm also incredibly excited to think that there could be something between us, to think that I might have the chance to bring him true happiness again.

When I started at the firm nearly eighteen years ago, at thirty-four I knew it was time to start looking for someone to spend my life with. It was a little late, actually, but I wasn't willing to settle, like some of my friends had. I didn't feel any clock ticking and was confident that it would happen when it happened. I wasn't very ambitious workwise either. I didn't necessarily have my sights set on moving up the corporate ladder. It was more that I thought I would work there for a few years, maybe fall in love, get married, have a child, work somewhere else. It was not my intention to become the longest-serving executive assistant at the firm (an award bestowed on me three years ago), and it was certainly not my intention to become an old maid. But at fifty-two years old, it seemed I was approaching just that. I had been having a one-sided affair with a married man for nearly two decades. Tonight it would either begin for real or it would end once and for all.

10

Dinner at the Four Seasons

By Arthur Winters, Attorney-at-Law
Age: 60

I was running late. Sherri hated it when I ran late. My plan was to be seated at the table and have her escorted in by Julian, the maître d'. The reason I was late is truly embarrassing — it's because I changed five times. Sherri had been slowly trying to make me look a little hipper, and for the most part I had been letting her try. I drew the line the week before at a pair of glasses from a place called Warby Parker. She said my current glasses made me look like Warren Buffett and I should be going for Warren Beatty. I was happy that for once I understood her points of reference but still did not succumb. I like my glasses; my wife picked them out.

You don't have to tell me how ridiculous this all sounds. I'm fully aware that I'm dating someone young enough to be my daughter and that we have very little in common. I mean, take tonight, for example.

This reservation at the Four Seasons for our anniversary was not selected for any of the wonderful reasons one would select the Four Seasons to celebrate a special occasion. It was selected because Sherri told me she's always wanted to go there, which made me happy until she added the reason why: 'Because my favorite *Real Housewives of New York* star had her wedding there on TV!' This made me laugh, more at myself than her, as I pictured the future negotiations that would have to take place every time the two of us ever watched television together.

I'm not a fool, although I know I must look like one. I don't much care. I lost the love of my life, and this girl Sherri is about as far from Marilyn as I could have gone — not one thing about her reminds me of my Marilyn. And that's fine with me.

I didn't set out to meet a girl as young as Sherri. I met her on a double blind date, when my recently divorced college roommate asked, 'This girl I'm seeing has a sister — want to double?'

I wasn't really ready to date, but I was beginning to fear that I might never be, so I agreed. I figured it was a good opportunity to get my feet wet — starting with a table for four would prove infinitely less intimidating than starting with a table for two. When I arrived, lo and behold, my friend's date was twenty years his junior, and her younger sister, Sherri, looked around the age of my daughters. I was a bit mortified, but I tried not to show it. Sherri didn't seem to notice or care. The wine flowed and the conversation was light and easy. I laughed out loud, and for the first time since Marilyn's death I was not awash in guilt about it. When the sister mentioned wanting to see Tony Bennett and Lady Gaga at Radio City and my friend offered to get us four tickets, I agreed. Sherri seemed so excited about it, and I liked them both, actually. Two dates led to a string of dinners and eventually overnights and brunches, and suddenly, without any plan or agenda, here I was, celebrating the four-month anniversary of that first date.

I arrived excited to show Sherri the Four Seasons, even if she wanted to see it for reasons I couldn't relate to. Julian greeted me with a regular's welcome and escorted me to my date, who was sitting at the bar with her back toward us. From behind I saw the little black dress that I'd had sent from Bloomingdale's — but the back wasn't Sherri's. The woman in the dress stood and turned to face me. She smiled a warm smile. She was stunning. She was Felicia.

I was speechless and doubly confused. Not

only was this not who I was expecting, but she looked so different from what I was used to. She greeted me with a kiss on the cheek.

'Hi, Arthur. You look so stunned to see me!' I was silent. 'I know, I look different than I do at the office.' Silent still. 'It's just a little makeup and — '

I got myself together and interrupted her. 'No, you look beautiful, Felicia. It's so nice to see you out . . . at night. I'm just not used to it.' I gave a quick look around the room, making sure Sherri wasn't sitting anywhere.

'Well, you're the one who invited me!' She laughed. 'You even sent me the dress — I assumed I should wear it!'

'Of course!' I took her arm, totally perplexed but, inexplicably, not at all unhappy about the turn of events. 'Let's go to our table.'

She grabbed her purse. 'Thank you. I've always wanted to come to the Four Seasons. You know, Jack Kennedy ate here the night Marilyn Monroe sang 'Happy Birthday' to him.'

'Really? I didn't know that.' I laughed at myself again. It was nice to get the reference this time.

'Don't worry,' she said, 'I don't expect you to sing like that to me.'

That's *right* — it was her birthday. I pieced

the whole mix-up together. Sherri would be furious.

Dinner was lovely, the food and wine superb, the conversation delightful, and eventually I began to ignore the constant vibrating of my phone in my pocket, which I knew must be Sherri getting angrier and angrier. We talked about anything and everything, but the thing that touched me most was the way she talked about Marilyn. 'Remember when Marilyn threw you that surprise party and I couldn't get you to leave the office?' Or, 'Remember how Marilyn always called Stanley-from-accounting's home-wrecking girlfriend by his ex-wife's name just to irritate her?' We laughed and laughed, and I realized that everyone around me had been scared to even mention Marilyn's name, let alone reminisce about her. Even my daughters avoided saying 'Mom.' It was as if everyone thought by bringing her up they would be reminding me of her, as if I forgot about her until someone said her name. It seemed that Felicia was the only one who knew that I was always thinking about her, that her name spoken out loud was a kind of comfort. Besides the meal and the wine and the conversation, I could not get over how pretty she was. This woman whom I had seen nearly every week-day for more than seventeen years was really very beautiful. I had just never stopped to sit across the table from her and look into her lovely blue eyes. I never even knew she had lovely blue eyes.

My phone was now vibrating on an almost continuous basis. I excused myself and called Sherri from the men's room. She was, as I expected, furious: furious over the 'old lady' cashmere shawl and the 'meaningless' card, furious over missing our anniversary, completely furious that I hadn't straightened out the situation the minute I saw Felicia, and over-the-top furious that Felicia had on *her* little black dress. I calmed her down as much as I could and promised to make the night a short one and come right over afterward. I said that we would reschedule and that I would make it twice as special. Just when I thought I was out of the woods she said, 'Make sure you tell her that I want that dress back.' Oh, boy. I could never do that.

I walked back to the table and a strange thing happened. I saw Felicia and I felt a little flutter in my stomach. I couldn't possibly have feelings for a woman I had worked beside for years. I chalked it up to my sweet tooth — the longing I always feel after a good meal for a little sugar. Hopefully the restaurant's signature cotton candy and the

Black Forest cake we had ordered for dessert would satiate me.

'So, besides dinner at the Four Seasons, what else is on your New York bucket list?' I asked.

'I've never seen a show at the Carlyle,' she said.

There was a pause — one I probably should have filled with an invitation to the Carlyle, but I didn't want to lead her on. She didn't seem to notice the lack of a forthcoming invitation and came right back with 'How about you?'

'Hmm . . . ' I thought. 'I've never walked across the Brooklyn Bridge.'

'Really?' she said. 'Well, that's an easy one. I know the best pizza place right on the other side — my treat!'

I smiled and agreed to her implicit suggestion. 'Sounds good.'

'How's Sunday?' she asked, her eyes sparkling. 'It's supposed to be beautiful out on Sunday.'

I should have said I had plans, but something stopped me.

11

An Out-of-Borough Experience

By Albert, Jeremy's Publicist
Age: 35 going on 60

As usual I woke up half an hour before my alarm, and as usual I ceremoniously waited in bed for it to go off. I don't know why I do that. I'm always hopeful that I'll doze off for a few more minutes' sleep, but I never do. If a shrink were to enter my head for that half an hour and observe the varied thoughts, memories, and forecasts that collide erratically into one another like balls on a pool table, they would certainly find substantial material for analysis. But today I focused my concern solely on the day ahead.

Hank called last night with what I thought was a pretty solid idea, and I was stressing because I hadn't been able to pull it off. Since no one had seen the girl's face, he thought it best that we hire our own girl, someone who looked like Bloomingdale's Girl, and substitute her in the new, staged paparazzi shots.

More control of the situation, he said. Hank was always looking for more control. He was worried about trusting Bloomingdale's Girl and was determined to firmly quash the rumors about Jeremy being gay. I was actually kind of proud of the way Jeremy declined to comment on the rumors, and kind of insulted by the way Hank said *gay* with the same intonation that he used for *Nazi sympathizer* or *Republican*. He never bothered to filter himself.

I called Jeremy to ask about us casting a new girl to be his beard, but he was adamant about sticking with Bloomingdale's Girl, whose name was apparently Natalie. He went on and on about some guy named Flip Roberts. I stopped listening after I realized his answer wasn't going to change, and concentrated on a game of Candy Crush Saga. Unsuccessful all around.

After spending the morning promising the pictures to a choice selection of news outlets, I headed to the photo shoot around noon. We were meeting at Astoria Studios in Queens. A friend at HBO hooked me up. They were shooting a red-carpet scene for a Lana Turner biopic and he said we could use the set during lunch. With the basic red carpet set up and the right Photoshopping, we'd have the perfect pictures and all our problems would be solved. Hank insisted that I pick up Jeremy in a car, but Jeremy wanted no part of that either. He said he was taking the subway to Queens. I don't know what's gotten into him; I didn't think he even knew how to take the subway, let alone to Queens. Images of him being swarmed by fans on the R train had me reaching for my first nibble of Xanax of the day. This whole thing had the potential to turn into a publicist's nightmare, and I was worried that it would blow up in our faces and ruin us both.

I met the beard outside the HBO lot. As soon as I saw her I understood what had gotten into Jeremy, or rather who: Natalie from Astoria. A cab pulled up around 1:15, and he emerged, late but in all his glory. He never failed to take my breath away. He had the hair of Ben Affleck, the smile of Robert Redford, the abs of Ryan Gosling, and the walk — the walk of Denzel Washington. I imagined that every gay man worth his weight in Kiehl's Ultra Facial Cream was filled with hope upon reading that he was one of us. I felt guilty for my part in disappointing them.

'Why is it that when I'm late it's like the whole city conspires against me?' he said, flashing that box-office smile. Lateness forgiven.

'What happened to the subway?' I asked

with a quick pat hello.

'I didn't have one of those cards.' He turned to Natalie. 'Where do you get one of those cards that you used the other day?'

She laughed and rolled her eyes. 'A MetroCard. It's very exclusive, I can't tell you.'

'She likes to tease,' he said, a goofy look on his face. Suddenly he frowned and, biting his bottom lip, asked if Hank was coming.

'Nope, it's just us,' I responded, causing him to release his lip and unleash that smile again. I melted. Natalie the beard spotted my reaction and gave me a knowing smirk as we entered the lot.

She was really quite refreshing. Wide-eyed like a kid in a candy shop. She didn't pretend for one second to be cool or unaffected. She oohed and aahed, and when my friend picked us up in a too-small golf cart, she peppered him with a million questions about the set and the studio, hopping right onto Jeremy's lap as if she'd been sitting there all her life. They certainly didn't seem like they'd met only a few days ago. This had rebound fling written all over it, which just increased the odds that this would all blow up in our faces. If Jeremy was going to love her and leave her, I needed to know, so that we could take measures to stop her from talking to the

103

press. There really is no rest for the publicist. When she went to change into her dress I came right out and asked him, 'So, you slept with her already?'

I fixed his tie as he made kissy faces at me, mocking my inquiry.

'Of course not, Albert. You know she's not my type.'

The photographer was testing the light and Jeremy asked him to take a picture of us. We smiled for the camera and he threw his arm around me. 'This guy is the love of my life!' He grabbed my face and gave me a big smooch, right on the lips!

I swatted him away. 'Okay, okay, quit fooling around — you know what Hank said about kissing dudes!'

'Whatever. Who needs Hank Haberman!' he shouted, full of bravado.

I laughed. We both knew the answer to that. But I appreciated how he treated me. He really was the best guy. He had this way about him that made you feel special, as if you were the star. Very few people recognized this in him; they couldn't see past the smile, the hair, the abs, and that cool strut of his to what was inside.

Natalie came back in the little black dress. She looked stunning. It was something different from Hollywood stunning. She lit up as she looked to Jeremy as though to say, 'Do I look okay?' There was something so sweet about her. She didn't seem to want anything from him.

'You know, actually, I can see you with a girl like her more than I ever could with your ex,' I said as he looked at her longingly.

'Me too, but she doesn't see me like that.'

'I find that hard to believe.'

'It's true. She's totally great, I really like her. But she's stuck on this ex of hers. I wish I could erase this whole week from my mind. Between being cheated on and now this rejection, I feel . . . horrible. Let's just get this over with.'

I snapped into action and made everything happen quickly. The last thing I needed on my hands was a depressed actor, and at this point I just felt bad for him. He was so much more fragile than he seemed. Within minutes we had the perfect shots, including plenty of close-ups where, with a little help from Photoshop, you wouldn't be able to tell the set backdrop from that at the premiere. I pretended I had pressing matters to discuss with Jeremy so he would have an excuse to leave with me instead of her, and we were out. Natalie looked disappointed, but I didn't care. Better she should be disappointed than my guy.

I was home by dinnertime, sitting on my couch with my boyfriend, eating takeout from Havana Shanghai, this delish Chinese-Cubano place up the block. All in all, the day was as painless as possible. Until 7:30 that night, when the pain came on tenfold, set to the ever-familiar *Entertainment Tonight* theme song.

You know the one — don't make me sing it.

'SEE EXCUSIVE VIDEO AS HEART-THROB JEREMY MADISON REVEALS HIS NOT-SO-SECRET LOVE, HIS PUBLICIST ALBERT STEIN, ONLY ON *ENTERTAINMENT TONIGHT!*'

Maybe you saw this coming. Obviously, I did not. Someone at the film studio had had a camera, caught Jeremy proclaiming his love for me, and sold it to *Entertainment Tonight*. While gays of the world rejoiced, I choked on my Cuban pork dumpling, my boyfriend threw a glass of very expensive wine in my face and stormed out, and Jeremy called my cell in a total panic.

'Oh my god, oh my god, oh my god! Someone filmed me saying 'Who needs Hank Haberman!'' He was completely irrational. 'I need Hank Haberman! *I need Hank Haberman!* He's going to drop me. I'm coming over!'

'Don't come over!' I said, dabbing at my face. 'You'll make it worse! We can't be seen together!' He'd already hung up. Reaching into my pocket for a Xanax to nibble on, I frantically texted him to stay away, but faster than the delivery boy from Havana Shanghai, Jeremy appeared at my door. I braced myself for more hysteria, but he seemed fine.

'You've calmed down,' I said suspiciously.

'There's a bunch of press and paparazzi in front of your building.' He shrugged. 'I got a chance to explain myself.'

'Thank god,' I said, feeling suddenly very calm myself. Phew. He had come to his senses, he'd cleared it all up, he'd told the world he wasn't really gay and he wasn't really in love with me. I stopped nibbling my Xanax. I sat on the couch and breathed. 'What did you say?'

He was very confident. 'I said, 'Hank Haberman is the best and most supportive agent there is, and clearly my comment was taken out of context.'' He beamed at me as though he'd just brokered world peace, when all he'd done was make things right with Hank. I popped the whole Xanax.

12

A Sunday Kind of Love

By Arthur Winters, Attorney-at-Law

I was late to meet Felicia because again I changed five times. I have seen this woman nearly daily for years and I was suddenly unreasonably consumed with worry over my appearance. It made no sense. This wasn't a date, just a walk over a bridge I had seen countless times. Never before, though, had I crossed it. There was a metaphor if ever I'd heard one.

Even though it wasn't a date, I hadn't told Sherri about it. I'd told her I had a business thing. She was so angry that I hadn't ended the Four Seasons mix-up before it started, how would she understand me actually planning to spend a Sunday with Felicia, or, as she called her, my washed-out secretary? I was beginning to wonder what I was doing myself. After all, I was lying; it was beginning to feel a bit like an affair, not that I had ever had one. Only I would cheat on a young blonde with my middle-aged assistant.

Though affairs with assistants are common-place. What am I talking about? This is not an affair! I promised myself to talk about business a little bit so that when I saw Sherri later I wouldn't have to lie. Well, not completely.

As my cab pulled over at City Hall, I saw Felicia on the sidewalk. She was wearing tennis shoes and capris. She looked . . . adorable. She approached the cab, and as I stepped out to pay she leaned over to give me a kiss hello. It was meant for my cheek, but I inadvertently turned my head and her lips ended up on mine. It was as if it unlocked something in both of us, and we began to kiss on the sidewalk like two teenagers with nowhere private to go. It seemed endless and was interrupted only by the cabbie shouting at me, 'Mister — your change!' I looked Felicia in the eye.

'Do you really want to walk across the bridge today?'

She couldn't even speak; she just shook her head. I turned to the cabbie. 'Keep the change. Take us to 57 Sutton Place, please,' I said, pulling her into the cab with me.

We made out the entire way. I don't even know how we composed ourselves enough to walk past my doorman. I pointed to the camera in the elevator and we stood in separate corners. When the doors opened it was like a race to my apartment. I fumbled with the keys and she grabbed them and opened the door for us. We barely made it to the bedroom, and by the time I touched her bare skin, she literally shuddered with desire. I had never thought about whether or not I was good in bed until I started dating someone half my age, and then I became suddenly and awkwardly aware. With Felicia it was as if I had magic hands. Every move I made, every touch was electric. And it was catching. It felt so good to make someone feel so good.

When it was over we lay staring at each other. I wondered what she was thinking. I knew what I was thinking. I was thinking, *I wonder if I'll ever feel that good again in my life.* And then we did it again. Twice. No Viagra. I was officially having an affair with my assistant.

Afterward we curled up under the covers and watched TV. She nuzzled into the crook of my arm as I switched channels. We both jumped at *The French Connection*. It had already started, but we'd both seen it before so we settled right in. We got to cross the Brooklyn Bridge that day after all, but with Popeye Doyle in his 1970 Buick.

'Did you know that this was the first

R-rated movie to win an Oscar?' Felicia said, adding, 'Depending how you look at it, though. Two years earlier *Midnight Cowboy* won, but it was rated X at the time. It was changed to R, so retroactively that's really first.' I had no idea she knew so much about movies. I looked at her wonderingly. What else was there I had to look forward to in getting to know her better? My look must have felt scrutinizing, as she suddenly seemed embarrassed. 'I know a lot of meaningless trivia about movies . . . I've taken a lot of movie classes.'

'I would love to take a movie class,' I said, trying to make her feel more comfortable. I was amazed. We'd just had the most explosive, uninhibited sex I could possibly imagine and I hadn't detected any embarrassment, yet this embarrassed her.

I looked over at the clock. It read five p.m. I panicked. How had it gotten so late? I was due to meet Sherri at Elio's at six for dinner with my girls. It was our family tradition to meet at Elio's every Sunday night. Marilyn and I started it when the girls were teenagers so that we'd be guaranteed some face time over the weekend, and it stuck. It grew from the four of us to six with the addition of my two sons-in-law, then to six and a high chair for my beautiful granddaughter. When

Marilyn died we kept it going. I think it was my girls' way of checking on me and getting me out of the house on weekends, when they worried, I think, that I would just shuffle around the apartment in my pajamas. The first time we walked in without Marilyn was brutal. There was our table in the corner, set for six and a high chair, as usual. One of my sons-in-law whispered in the maître d's ear and we watched as a busboy removed the sixth chair. Not one of us uttered a word that night. Even the baby seemed to sense our pain and just sat there sucking ziti from her little fingers.

Over the past few months with Sherri my Sundays have been very different. My old Sundays with Marilyn involved reading the *Times* cover to cover, maybe taking a walk in the park, and usually seeing a movie, either at the theater or right here in the very bed I was lying in with Felicia. Sundays with Marilyn were blissful and familiar. Kind of like this Sunday had turned out, though now there was the minor addition of my having suddenly become Don Juan at sixty — a whole new definition for sexagenerian! Sundays with Sherri, on the other hand, usually involved brunch at some 'amazing' new place downtown with an organic menu featuring artisanal cheese, heirloom tomatoes, and, if I was lucky, the occasional gluten-free doughnut. I once made a joke about Sherri's generation speaking about gluten the way mine spoke about crack, and was stared at blankly by her six young friends. These boozy brunches were followed either by a shopping spree or, occasionally, a gallery visit. But no matter how we filled our Sundays, they all ended with me heading uptown alone to get ready for dinner with my family while she moped because she wasn't invited. I could hardly tell her the real reason that I didn't want her to come: I couldn't bear for her to sit in Marilyn's seat, or the looks from the staff at Elio's when they saw I was dating someone closer to my daughters' age than my own. But I had an ironclad excuse; the rules of Sunday night dinners had been set long ago, as soon as our oldest started dating: no significant others until they were engaged. We still met plenty of boyfriends over the years, but Sunday night was family night, and there were no exceptions — until the Four Seasons mix-up, that is. When I'd been unable to produce the little black dress, I had attempted to make up for it with an invitation to Sunday night dinner at Elio's. Don't ask me why I felt the need to keep pretending with Sherri. I just couldn't bear to disappoint her, although I knew that it was coming, and that it would ultimately be for the best. But tonight wasn't the right time to end things with her. So I had one hour to get Felicia out of my apartment as chivalrously as possible, shower, and get to the restaurant where a woman that I had nothing in common with would sit in my wife's seat while my daughters faked happiness for me and the waiters rolled their eyes at the cliché I had become.

13

#ThisWasSoNotThePlan

By Sophie Stiner, Brown Graduate
Age: Nearly 23

I never saw this coming, at least not anywhere in the pages of my carefully mapped-out life plan. According to that, the year after college graduation was to be filled with after-work meet-ups with old friends and new colleagues in smart outfits chosen from my modest but stylish closet. In that plan, said closet would be found either in my shared Junior 4 in a part-time-doorman building uptown or in my own studio walk-up downtown. In my daydreams it was never found, as it now stands, in my childhood bedroom, partially co-opted by my mother's off-season wardrobe.

I have always been a planner in a family of non-planners. I grew up on the Upper East Side of Manhattan and began my education at PS 6, the local public elementary school with a reputation for being all that. It was fine, but by the third grade I had started

115

downloading applications to Dalton, Trinity, and Columbia Prep and leaving them next to the coffee machine for my parents to peruse with their morning brew. When that didn't work, I tried sticking them right in their briefcases, and then in their gym bags.

My father, David, the product of Upper West Side Jewish political activists, dismissed them outright at first: 'I went to public school and it worked out fine for me!' My mother, Sheila, the daughter of conservative black schoolteachers from Buffalo, was a little more understanding: 'She seems to really want this, David. It can't hurt to just tour the schools.'

Actually it can, and that was exactly what I was counting on. Once we toured the first one, even my liberal dad couldn't deny that private school was the best place for me.

I wowed the admissions committee, asking calculated questions like 'What community-service opportunities will be available to me at Dalton?' and 'Would it be possible for me to start a knitting club to make baby booties for Chinese orphans?' Between that and my stellar grades on the entrance exams, I was able to make up for the fact that my parents had both graduated from state schools, leaving me legacy-less and therefore not a shoo-in for the Ivy League. Top-tier college acceptances sit like a pot of gold at the end of the New York City private school rainbow; all the touring parents (except for mine) pretend not to care, claiming to be more interested in inclusion and diversity, but really the bottom line is how many kids got into Ivies last year.

As soon as I was accepted to Dalton I changed my focus to the next goal in life — the Ivy League. I was in eighth grade, and starting the next year everything would count. I met my new classmates and sized them up one by one. Since it was a numbers game, my legacy-less acceptance to an Ivy League college depended heavily on who in my class had a legacy and where. I found casual ways to ask my classmates where their parents had gone to college and wrote down the results in a little notebook I kept under my bed so my parents wouldn't find it and send me to a shrink. In retrospect, it's unfortunate they never found it — I probably could have benefited from a little therapy. Though of course they had noticed that my competitive nature was a bit obsessive. Even if they hadn't, it was pointed out to them at nearly every teacher conference.

By Christmas of ninth grade I had created a detailed spreadsheet of the competition, with Ivy League schools listed across the top and classmates who were legacies of them underneath. In the end the tally included a whopping seven legacies from my original first choice, University of Pennsylvania, and, even more discouraging, nine from the easiest to get into, Cornell. As I was not in the academic league of Harvard, Yale, Princeton, or Columbia, this left me to choose between Dartmouth (2) and Brown (3). I studied the acceptance rates to those two schools from Dalton over the previous five years — all good — and then looked at the candidates themselves. The Dartmouth legacies were strong, both of them girls, one black like me, but the Brown legacies were all boys, and sniffling, boring white boys to boot. I ordered a Brown sweatshirt online and set my mind and my every move over the next three years to my future admission to Brown University. As you can see from my byline, I was accepted.

At Brown my drive to compete changed dramatically, in that I quickly realized I no longer could. Everyone had my stellar SAT scores, and if I had knitted enough baby booties to cover every orphaned foot in Beijing, population 11 million, then the girl across the hall had knitted enough to cover every orphaned foot in Shanghai, population 14 million. I spent my first semester trying to be the best, but somewhere in the late winter, as the snow began to melt, my focus shifted from realizing achievements to managing disappointment. I gave up on the idea of being at the top and ended up four years later graduating smack in the middle of my class, with no idea what was next. Unceremoniously dumped into the world, and without my usual clearly charted path, I took my double concentration in comparative literature and art history and headed home to NYC to take my place in the postgraduate abyss. And since I was not yet gainfully employed, I moved back in with Sheila and David.

Everyone I knew seemed to be landing jobs, getting paid, and doing lots of fun and interesting things with their paychecks. I, on the other hand, was going to one unsuccessful job interview after another and was totally broke. My parents had laid down hard-and-fast ground rules when I moved back in, and those rules did not include money for fun or interesting things. 'We will provide a roof over your head and food on the table, but we are done subsidizing your life,' they told me. Their parents hadn't given them a cent after college, and, as they loved to remind me, they'd also had student loans to pay off.

Just as the rejection was beginning to really take hold on my psyche, I stumbled onto an instant ego-booster while browsing through Bloomingdale's. Often, to cheer myself up after interviews, I'll get off the subway at 59th Street and exit into the basement of the store. Sometimes I'll try a new perfume; sometimes I'll get a free makeover, though not totally free, since I pay the price in guilt for not making a purchase. One day back in September when I was dressed in an interview suit with a particularly good makeup job, I bumped into an old Dalton classmate, Bitsy Bouvier. She too was dressed in a suit and looking pretty fabulous. She was always a step behind me at Dalton and went to a little Ivy — Hamilton, I believe. She squealed when she saw me as if we'd met crossing the Ponte Vecchio, as opposed to in the department store we'd both been frequenting since we could walk. 'Sophie, I love your hair! You look so . . . cool!'

I couldn't help but laugh at the absurdity. If she only knew my new hairstyle was a DIY special. The week before, my mother had caught me staring at myself in the mirror, forlorn. She's more of a softy than my dad, and sometimes I play on it. So when she asked me what was wrong, I saw an opportunity.

'It's my hair, Mom — I don't know what to do with it. You know I've been trying so hard to get a job and I can't even afford to get my hair straightened anymore.' I welled up — it's a talent of mine, I can do it on cue. She had to understand, she had the same hair. Although she wears hers like some kind of badge of honor. She took my hand and led me to her bedroom. *Oh, good, she's going to give me a little cash*, I thought. Cash would be nontraceable; my father would never know. She'd done the same thing two weeks earlier when I needed new interview shoes. But this time she sat me down in front of the mirror and pulled out a pair of barber's shears.

'No way, Mom!' I immediately protested.

'Embrace it,' she said. 'You're not going to want to spend half your salary on your hair when you get a job, either!' She added, 'Come on, I'll make you look cool.' We both laughed. *Cool* has never been a word you would use to describe me. Practical, driven, competitive, and, more recently, mediocre, lost, and unemployable — but never cool.

'What the hell,' I said, relenting. 'I'll wear it ironically.' According to Bitsy Bouvier's compliment, it was working for me.

'How are you? What have you been up to?' she asked, doubtless expecting to hear a success story, since I'd been one of the stars of our high school class.

'Keeping it real,' I responded with a smile. What I should have said was keeping it real cheap.

'Where are you working?' And there it was,

the question I had come to dread.

'You look fabulous — where are you working?' I countered.

'Goldman Sachs!' *Goldman Sachs?* She didn't even go to an Ivy League school! Maybe I should have gone to a little Ivy — less pressure and more room to flourish. I was beginning to question every decision I'd ever made.

'That's great,' I said, adding a bit viciously, 'I'm surprised they let you out of the office at all, let alone to traipse through Bloomingdale's at five-thirty on a weekday!'

She laughed. 'I'm treating myself to a new dress — I'm going to the ballet tonight with my boyfriend and his parents.'

A *job* and a *boyfriend*, with parents who attended the ballet? I nearly imploded from jealousy. But instead I lied. 'That's funny. I'm here to buy a new bathing suit, because I'm going to the Ocean Club next weekend with *my* boyfriend and *his* parents!'

She looked sincerely happy for me. God, I'm awful. She whipped out her phone to take a selfie of us. I leaned in as she put her arm around my shoulder. Snap.

'I'll Instagram it! What should the caption be? Got it! #TwoDaltonWorkingGirls. So cute — I'll tag you. Where did you say you work again?'

'Sotheby's,' I answered, as quickly as if she had asked my shoe size.

She pecked away on her phone: #Dream-jobs #Sothebys #GoldmanSachs.

And that's how it began.

With each new like on Instagram I felt less like a loser and more like the twentysome-thing success with a great boyfriend and a job at Sotheby's that I'd told Bitsy I was. I checked Instagram all night, and by the time Bitsy Bouvier was watching the last plié at Lincoln Center, the photo had 179 likes. One hundred and seventy-nine people thought I looked fabulous — possibly even cool — and had a dream job at Sotheby's!

I was instantly addicted.

By the next morning people were on to liking the hot matchachino that Bitsy had for breakfast and I found myself feeling like a total loser again. I didn't even know what a matchachino was.

With nothing to do, I wandered back over to Bloomingdale's and ended up drifting through the bathing suit department. It was empty and a saleswoman approached. 'Are you going somewhere warm?' she asked.

'Yes, to the Bahamas with my boyfriend and his family.' The lie came out again without my even thinking about it. If I couldn't have it all, I could at least *imagine* having it all, couldn't I?

She pulled out a beautiful Eres bikini. 'Try this.'

I headed for the dressing room. She soon knocked on the door with a few more suits for me to try. I fell in love with an orange Norma Kamali with lavender flowers.

'It looks great on you!' she said as I timidly opened the changing room door. I looked at the tag — $185, just for the bottom.

'It's a little expensive for me,' I said. Even when fantasizing, I was pragmatic. I'm so not cool.

'Well, you look great. Give me your phone — I'll take a picture for you to send to your boyfriend. Maybe he'll buy it for you.'

I want to be able to buy my own Norma Kamali suit, I thought as I handed her my phone and posed for a photo. She looked at it and laughed.

'Check this out — with that picture of palm trees behind you, it looks like you're already in the Bahamas!' As she left she added, 'Here's my card. Tell your BF that if he really loves you, he should call me for that suit!'

I sat down and looked at the picture. I looked great in the suit, and she was right, it did look like I was in the Bahamas. I couldn't help myself. I posted it on Instagram

— #ItsBetterInTheBahamas. There were seven likes by the time I hooked my bra, double that by the time I zipped my jeans. And in the all-caps word of my first comment, I was once again AMAZING!!!!!!!

My friends began texting me — 'You're in the Bahamas?' 'Who are you with?' 'You got vacation time from Sotheby's already?'

I invented a boyfriend, Charles, to go along with my dream job and my fabulous coolness. To avoid any risk of being found out and having to lie to people's faces, I turned down all invitations, excusing myself on the grounds of prior commitments related to said boyfriend, job, and fab coolness. The more excuses I made, the more pictures I posted to back them up. The busier I looked, the more popular and sought-after I became and the more likes I racked up. Every like fed my suffering ego. It was a dizzying cycle, and pretty soon I was on Instagram all the time, managing my pretend life.

Bloomingdale's seemed to be the perfect resource for all things Instagram-likable. A tight forty-five-degree-angled selfie shot in the housewares department holding my cool new immersion mixer: 198 likes; napping on six on my new Calvin Klein bedding, photo-enhanced with Beyoncé's favorite filter, Valencia: 243 likes; rushing to work with just a peek of my new Hermès bag in the corner, Lo-Fi filter: 372 likes and one covetous comment: *Is that the new Berline bag?* #SoJel.

It became a full-time job. Every Monday I would check the New York Social Diary calendar and map out my fictional appearances for the week. I would turn down an invitation to dinner with a 'Sorry, opening-night gala at the Met!' Which I then had to follow with a photo of me in a Carolina Herrera gown from the fancy designer floor, with the always flattering Mayfair filter: a whopping 379 likes! I attended all the right charitable events in all the right designers — Gucci, Galliano, and Gabbana — and just last week I wore the most perfect little black Max Hammer, which Natalie, the saleswoman, told me was *the* dress of the season, to the New York Public Library benefit. No filter, 432 likes, one regram.

That Max Hammer dress helped me make an awesome connection in the art world; maybe this whole fake-life thing could help me get a real life after all. Apparently Thea Baxter, who graduated from Brown a few years before me and now works at Christie's, is one of my *900* new Instagram followers. On one of my many lazy Monday mornings she called me (Yes! Called me!) to say she had seen my Max Hammer post and had been searching all over for me at the library benefit, but to no avail. I couldn't help but chuckle to myself: while I was managing my virtual life by matching up the hottest NYC event with the hottest look at Bloomie's, she was looking for me IRL. She went on to ask me about my responsibilities at Sotheby's but, lucky for me, quickly turned her sights to what she really wanted to know: my salary.

'That Max Hammer dress you were wearing was gorgeous. You killed it. What are they paying you over at Sotheby's?'

I hemmed and hawed, mumbling something about not wanting to talk about money, as I Googled starting salaries at Sotheby's.

'C'mon, I'll tell you what my starting salary was at Christie's,' she pleaded.

'Fifty-two thousand,' I lied, adding a few grand to the Google results to annoy her.

'Are you off today?' she asked.

I paused and contemplated my two choices. 'Yes,' I answered and held my breath.

'Oh, they give you Columbus Day off?' she whined, obviously at work.

I guess it's October, I thought, realizing I had never checked to see what was new on Netflix this month, I looked around my bed for the remote.

'You know, we're looking to expand our Asian Contemporary department before the new year. Would you consider a move?'

I stopped looking for the remote. 'I wrote my senior thesis on Japanese avant-garde!'

'I know — I've done my research.'

I was surprised.

'I'll invite you to our Christmas party and introduce you to my boss.'

'That would be wonderful. I'm definitely interested,' I answered.

We hung up and I felt the first glimmer of hope for my future. I opened up Instagram and took a selfie, sitting on my bed in the room I'd grown up in, eating Oreos from the package. My signed poster of the Spice Girls was slightly visible in the background. I wrote #hopeful. It was my first honest post in forever. And then, of course, I deleted it.

14

Come Monday

By Felicia (aka Arthur Winters' Executive Assistant)

I was glad Arthur was honest with me. He came right out and told me that I had to leave because he was meeting Sherri and the girls at Elio's. I mean, I guess I had assumed that it was over with Sherri or he wouldn't have asked me to the Four Seasons to begin with, but people have strange rules about dating nowadays. I guess Arthur was following today's rules, not the old-fashioned ones we grew up with. Truth be told, I was too happy to care, even if I had, after all these years of avoiding it, become the other woman.

Our relationship was illicit all around. Office protocol says that employees cannot date each other. Partners can certainly not date their secretaries. Secretary — I said it again. It's become a bad word, taboo, along with *stewardess* and *garbage man. Assistants* — partners cannot date their *assistants*. I don't consider myself to be old-fashioned, yet much of my lingo dates me, and I don't get half the words these young associates and their assistants use: *bandwidth, wheelhouse, low-hanging fruit*. I wish they'd just say what they mean. As I ate my buttered sesame bagel and glanced at the girl in the next cubicle eating tofu and quinoa out of a bamboo bowl, with chopsticks, I was again thankful to be working for someone of my generation. God, I hope I didn't blow that by sleeping with the boss.

It would probably be quite difficult for me to get another job at my age, and anyway, I didn't really want to. I loved it here for reasons that went far beyond seeing Arthur every day. Even if he were to become my boyfriend and I were to see him every night, I'd still want to keep it a secret until I knew it was worth what I would need to give up. Oh god. I was really getting ahead of myself. What if Arthur were to walk in, call me into his office, and say, *Felicia, I'm sure we can both agree that yesterday was a one-time thing and we should just put it behind us?* I had to prepare myself for that. How could I think it was anything more than lust? I tried to plan ahead to avoid being blindsided. I would go along with it: *Of course, Arthur. I was going to say the same thing. I'm so glad you said it first.*

I looked at the clock. He was late. He was never late. Oh my god. He wasn't coming in because he couldn't face me. How could I have let myself go like that? I was mortified. Why hadn't I controlled myself? I should've been smarter, I should never have let any of this happen. When he'd asked if I still wanted to cross the bridge, I should have said, *Yes, Arthur, I was looking forward to it.* He must think I'm easy. Me — easy.

The elevator dinged, and in walked Arthur Winters. It was a sight I had seen five mornings a week for nearly eighteen years. And I'm embarrassed to say that for most of that time it was a sight that caused my stomach to flutter and my knees to wobble ever so slightly as I stood to follow him into his office to go over his schedule. Today my stomach fluttered and my knees wobbled, but it wasn't just from love, it was from fear as well. Before we'd consummated this fantasy of mine, the notion of Felicia and Arthur kind of kept me going, in the romance department at least. It was what I dreamed about when falling asleep at night. Now that very notion might be dead.

As I followed him into his office I braced myself for what might come out of his mouth. I closed the door behind me and steadied myself against it. I knew I wouldn't make it

131

without physical support. He didn't even bother to hang up his coat. He just came right out with it. 'Felicia,' he said. I pushed my hands against the door and held on. I wasn't sure if I was capable of speech, but the word *yes* somehow came out of my mouth. He came closer and said my name again, this time as if he had something important to say. He stood right in front of me. 'Felicia — I . . . ' And then he kissed me. He pinned me against the door and kissed me with as much passion as he had yesterday. Maybe more. By the time he reached his hand under my skirt my anticipation was evident. Today I was embarrassed by it until I saw his reaction. As he touched me there he smiled the slowest, warmest smile of satisfaction I had ever seen on his beautiful worn face. I couldn't believe that smile was all for me. We slid down and in purposeful silence made love on the floor of his office. It was different from yesterday. It was slow, in the way that you sometimes take your time with each bite of a decadent dessert. Our eyes were locked on each other's the entire time. When it was over a tear ran down my cheek. He kissed it but didn't ask why I was crying. He knew. He knew that even though we'd had sex three times before, and even though we were lying on his office floor, we had just made love for the first time.

And it was beautiful. We sat up and he looked at me, his eyes sparkling with the first happiness I had seen there in a long time. We smiled at each other for what seemed like hours. But the growing bustle of the office outside as it got closer to ten brought us back to reality.

'What else is on the schedule for today?' he asked, barely stifling a laugh.

I laughed too, stood up, adjusted my skirt, and started to read him his schedule. It was a busy day.

15

Misadventures of the Ostrich Detective Agency

By Andie Rand, Private Detective

It had been one week since Caroline Westmont had visited my office and I had not one shred of evidence against her husband. He was the most artfully deceptive cheater I had yet to come across. I went through my entire arsenal of weapons, from mobile trackers to encryption software, and got nothing in return. He was almost too clean. It only made me more suspicious.

The practicalities of his infidelity were as untraceable as they come. There were no clandestine meetings, or e-mails or texts back and forth confirming where these clandestine meetings would occur. He had a regular session with his masseuse every Tuesday at eleven o'clock, at her office; he was cheating by appointment, which was the perfect cover. No chance photos of his naked body through a hotel window. No fake out-of-town conferences to expose. Other than the cheater, there was only one person who had the evidence I needed, so I made an appointment to see this masseuse myself.

I was confident that given an hour alone with Anna I'd be able to get something useful out of her. Getting stuff out of people was kind of my specialty. Ever since I was a kid people liked to confess to me. At sleep-away camp my friends would call me the Catskill Confessional because of the long, drawn-out letters I received from my home friends chronicling their summertime sins. It's like they forgot that come September I would see them in person and be able to hold them accountable. Not that I ever did; I was never very judgmental.

I arrived for my scheduled massage a few minutes early. It was in a partially converted apartment, not a proper office, though all the necessary framed documentation was on the walls. On the one hand it was legit, on the other the perfect place to cheat. The scenario that Caroline had presented, an affair conveniently divided into weekly seventy-five-minute sessions, was completely plausible. She said that John had first come here under the direction of his physician for back problems. I wondered how many affairs to date had been covered by Obamacare.

A woman leaving the inner sanctum

interrupted my thought. I was up next. A few minutes later Anna appeared. I was slightly taken aback to see that she looked close to my age. She reached out a strong hand to greet me. I suddenly felt a bit uncomfortable, as undercover work isn't really my thing. Plus this undercover work meant being naked in front of a stranger. I took a deep breath and reminded myself that I was doing this for Caroline, for all the wives out there whose husbands are screwing the masseuse. I followed Anna into a darkened room that smelled like lilacs. She told me to undress and get up on the table facedown, then left the room again. I kept my thong on, so as not to feel completely vulnerable, and slid under the white sheet. I was glad to be facedown — much easier for me to interrogate her from that direction.

She came back in and turned on a white-noise machine set to ocean waves. I thought about how badly I needed to relax and considered forgetting the investigation, taking this massage just for me and making another appointment for next week. But I thought of poor Caroline. She had told me that today was their anniversary and the thought of smiling and making nice all night was killing her. She said that she was close to just giving up and leaving him without the proof she needed to break the prenup. Twelve years of marriage, and she would leave with half of what he earned as a professor at Columbia. The injustice made me rally.

I came at Anna from every angle, from 'So, are you married?' to 'Do you feel weird massaging a man?' all the way to 'Has a client ever made a pass at you?' She answered no to every question. That's it — no opinions, no elaborations. Just no. She wasn't the chatty type, and it didn't seem like any confession would be forthcoming. As she worked on the knot in my right shoulder I tried to think of questions requiring more than one-word answers. But it was infinitely easier to relax than to concentrate. Done with my shoulders, she put more oil on her hands and came around to the side of the table. She rubbed her hands briskly together and worked on my left hip from above and below. As she did, she pressed her hand into the scar from the emergency C-section I'd had when I gave birth to my twins nearly eight years ago. Within seconds I found myself crying.

She noticed my tears. 'I'm sorry,' she said. 'Did I hurt you?'

I shook my head. She hadn't at all. And it wasn't the memory of the C-section that made me cry, though remembering the moment when my birthing plans had gone

137

out the window as I was rushed away for surgery had certainly brought tears to my eyes before.

No, I was crying because I suddenly realized that hers were the only hands aside from my own ever to have touched that scar. I had my girls for both of us, Derek and me. I was brave as it was happening, and equally brave during the months of healing that followed. But Derek always looked at my scar with slight distaste, as if the sacrifice had been mine alone. I wished then and I wished now that I'd married the kind of man who would have loved my scar. Who would have traced it with the tips of his fingers before kissing me and telling me that I was beautiful. I don't remember Derek telling me that once after the twins were born. Some scars never heal.

I was silent for the rest of the session, but my mind wasn't. I wondered if I would ever be part of a couple again. I had yet to meet a man that I trusted enough to even show my scar to. I'd had a few flings right after my divorce, but getting close to another man wasn't on my divorce to-do list. That's what I call it. After my divorce I made a list of all the things I'd ever thought of wanting to do when I was married that I never could do. You know, those illicit thoughts that run through the mind of every married woman about things they never got around to before they jumped the broom. I married young, basically going from my parents' home to my marital one. I didn't get much out of my system pre-wedded bliss, and unlike my ex, I wouldn't have dreamed of breaking my vows. My only dream was to have a happy, loving marriage. When that failed, I needed to find an upside, and doing all the things a married woman can't do was the only upside I could think of. And it really did help. For those of my clients whose cases result in divorce, I always recommend the divorce to-do list.

The first step, as I advise all future divorcées, is to sell the engagement ring and take a trip with the proceeds. My ring, a two-and-a-half-carat empire cut, didn't yield as much as I expected — it turned out the ring was as flawed as the man who gave it to me — but when I threw in the diamond wedding band, the spoils of my spoiled marriage got me through the first item on my list: a solo trip to Sicily. There I spent the week with a beautiful Italian, the second item on my list. He didn't speak English, but we managed to communicate just fine. Back home I followed up that decadent week with a couple of one-night stands and a three-month fling with a much younger jazz musician whom I met on his cigarette break (yes, I briefly took up smoking again) outside of Minton's jazz club in Harlem. He played the bass nearly as well as he played me, and I learned that even with all that extramarital practice, Derek wasn't a very good lover. These flings were just for fun, though. I never introduced anyone to my girls, and mostly only saw the men when the girls were with Derek. I didn't need a boyfriend to make me happy, just them — to me the best nights involved the three of us seeing a Broadway musical or even just singing along to one at home in our pajamas. I was happiest when I was with them, and soon I tossed my list in the trash, satisfied that I had sowed my oats.

Concentrating on forming my company as opposed to lasting relationships was a healthy move for me. Many newly divorced women take a different approach. They want to find a new man straightaway. I don't think one way is better than the other. It may seem like my approach renders me the stronger, braver woman, but I'm not so sure. Those women who get right back on the horse seem pretty brave to leave themselves vulnerable again. I couldn't even take off my thong for a masseuse.

My thoughts had distracted me, and before I knew it my time on the table was up. I left the appointment feeling slightly enlightened about myself and completely unenlightened about John Westmont. As I stood by the subway entrance on the corner of 59th and Lex, the tension began to seep back into my neck and shoulders. I called CC, who was actually at the office on a Sunday, to admit my failure. She was comforting and suggested that she take a crack at John Westmont herself. Every now and then, when all else fails and we are sure of someone's infidelity but lacking proof, we resort to an entrapment scenario. I'm not particularly proud of this aspect of our business, but sometimes it's necessary to use a few tricks to catch a rat in the act. We'll usually hire a younger woman for the job, to maximize the temptation factor, but since Anna was close to my age, and since Caroline said that John wasn't the college-coed type, I knew that CC would do for the part. She had played temptress on a few occasions when an older woman seemed to fit the bill. She'd acted in college and was more attractive than most women half her age. She didn't mind doing it, but I wouldn't take her up on it. I knew her husband, who was still out of work and feeling increasingly demoralized, was not a fan of his wife's fake-seducing a stranger, even if it was paying the bills. I can't say I blame him.

I walked down the stairs to the subway, stopping just before the entrance so as not to lose the call. 'We'll just hire someone older,' I said understandingly, even though I couldn't remember what it was like to have someone around to care whether I fake-seduced all of the Upper West Side.

'Too bad you don't have the guts,' she taunted. We both knew I didn't. 'Hold on!' she said, suddenly sounding alarmed. 'Where did you say you were?'

'At the subway station by Bloomingdale's,' I told her, and she gasped.

'So is John Westmont.'

My eyes darted around the subway platform. I couldn't see anyone who looked like the man in the photographs.

'It's packed, but I don't see him,' I said, scanning the crowd. A train came, and nearly everyone on the platform got on. After it pulled away I asked, 'Is he still here?'

'Yup,' CC responded. 'I bet he's in Bloomingdale's.'

I thought about Caroline, about myself, about all the people being cheated on all over town right at this very moment. All of a sudden it seemed imperative that I find and catch this one cheater today. My adrenaline kicked in and I announced my plan: 'I'm going to seduce John Westmont myself.'

'It's a big store, Andie. You're gonna have to find him first.'

'Maybe I can narrow it down. I bet he's buying Caroline an anniversary gift. Trust a cheater to wait until the day of. Just keep your eye on the screen and call me back if he leaves.'

I knew it would take a while, but Derek had the kids tonight — he even had Franny, our dog, so I had nowhere to be. With anniversary gifts in mind, I started my search in the jewelry department. No John Westmont. Figures — he was probably in housewares, buying her a vacuum cleaner. I covered the handbag and perfume departments quickly and headed to the escalator. I knew the store like the back of my hand. I grew up in the suburbs, and Bloomingdale's was the first place in the city my friends and I were allowed to go on our own. It's where I was measured for my first bra and bought my first lip gloss. It really is like no other store in the world. As I made my way up, I told myself that if I didn't find him I'd go get frozen yogurt on seven as a consolation — win-win.

I reached the third floor about twenty minutes into my search. I called CC to check that he was still in the store. Just as she answered, I spotted him.

'I have eyes on him!' I whispered, in full detective mode.

'Keep me in your ear and I'll tell you what to say.'

'I've got this,' I said, and hung up. I wanted to do this sans CC de Bergerac.

John Westmont was standing in the middle of the ladies' dress department with an armful of dresses. He began laying them out on a table shoulder to shoulder as I approached. I thought quickly and came up with my first line.

'That's a lot of dresses. Are you outfitting a black-tie women's basketball team?' I said with a confident smile. I thought it was pretty witty. He looked up, confused.

'Do you work here?' he asked.

I shook my head, having that awkward feeling you get when you speak to a stranger and don't get a warm response.

'Do I know you?'

'I don't think so,' I replied, thinking I might have blown it. My mind raced, trying to think of something to say to cut the weirdness. He seemed to smell the air.

'You smell familiar,' he said, blushing.

Of course I do, I thought. *I smell like the lavender massage oil that your mistress rubs on you. Cheating dog.* Maybe this would work in my favor, remind him of Anna and sex.

He sheepishly looked down at the dresses. 'My anniversary's coming up and I'm trying to buy my wife a dress,' he explained, sighing in a way that seemed heartfelt.

'I can help,' I said.

'Would you?' He seemed relieved. He had no idea that his wife was on to him. This was the part of my job I liked best — knowing something the dishonest spouses didn't.

'Sure, but a dress is a really hard thing to buy for another person. Why don't you get her something she doesn't need to try on, like jewelry?' I said. The whole time I was thinking that this was an odd MO for a philanderer, talking about a gift for his wife. But I do hear that certain women are more attracted to married men, and I guess he had to explain the fact that he was shopping in the women's dress department.

'I know what you mean, but it's our twelve-year anniversary,' he said, as if that explained the need for a dress.

'So?' I asked.

'Oh, so, the twelve-year anniversary is silk. It's a less-known thing than paper or silver, but I looked it up and I thought it was a nice idea.'

It *was* a nice idea. Very caring, for a lying wretch. 'How about a silk scarf?' I asked.

'Well, actually I have another reason,' he

said. 'My wife and I are very different.' *Here it comes*, I thought. The old 'my wife doesn't understand me' routine. He continued. 'She likes to go out nearly every night — she's very social. And I'm more of a homebody. Lately she's been saying I don't listen to her wants.' He stopped and looked at me, a puzzled look on his face. 'I don't know why I'm telling you all this.' *I do*, I thought. *So you can use the caring-husband-with-a-distant-wife routine to pick me up.* The sympathy play. Pathetic.

He continued. 'I want to show her that I'm listening and will go out more. So I want to buy her a dress she can go out in. With me. Like a romantic gesture.' He picked up one of the dresses and asked, 'How about this one?' He held it up next to me. Then, looking me up and down in a way that made me blush involuntarily, he said, 'Actually, you look to be about the same size as my wife. Can I hold it up against you?'

He'd picked out a really beautiful dress — the kind of dress you would try on just for kicks and then buy because you couldn't bear to leave it behind.

'Want me to try it on?' I offered.

'Would you?'

He took the bait, and I took the little black dress and headed for the dressing room, channeling my inner Mata Hari (although I think her seductions and spying ended in her execution).

'Can you zip me? It's hard to reach . . . ' I whispered, testing out my charm in the dressing-room mirror. The dress was gorgeous. Looking at myself in it made me long for somewhere glamorous to go. I didn't dress up much anymore. I worked a lot, and anyway, I just wasn't invited to many things where one would wear something elegant like this. This dress felt like it was from another era. Not old-fashioned — timeless. And I was dateless. Maybe we made a good pair, this timeless dress and dateless me. Maybe I should tell him it was ripped and buy it for myself, I thought. Coming back to reality for a moment, I had to admit to myself that I didn't feel comfortable wearing something so look-at-me. Since I was an unmarried woman with a circle of mostly married friends, it seemed like the only people I would be calling out to in a dress like this were other women's husbands. *Other women's husbands!* Eye on the prize, Andie! I put on the used dressing-room heels to up the ante on my sex appeal. I checked myself in the mirror and went out to show Caroline's cheating husband. I couldn't believe what I was doing. But the dress made me feel so confident, so seductive — it made me feel like everything would go my way.

John was sitting on a chair eating almonds. He barely noticed me. I guess I wasn't such a great seductress after all — I had to cough just to get his attention. For a shameless philanderer he sure had some less-than-predatory methods. Either that or I had totally lost my mojo. Though wearing that dress, I didn't feel like I'd lost any mojo at all.

'Want an almond?' he offered.

I did. I hadn't eaten since lunch.

'Did you ever notice that when you bite into raw almonds it sounds like the first few notes to the song 'Build Me Up Buttercup'?'

It may have been one of the strangest questions I'd ever heard, but it made me smile. I'm a really good judge of character, and it didn't seem like this man had any interest in picking me up. Not with a nutty line like that, I thought, making myself cringe at my corny joke. The twins called it 'mom humor.' I asked him for another almond and thought about his question as I listened to the crunch. I agreed, and he seemed happy that I got it.

A saleswoman approached us cautiously. 'Are you buying that dress?' she asked. But her tone was slightly off — it almost sounded like she didn't want us to buy it. Maybe she wanted it for herself? I wouldn't blame her.

'I'm not sure. Are we?' I asked the man, who I was starting to believe really was just looking for the perfect present for his wife. He explained to the saleswoman that he needed something silk for his twelfth anniversary. She discouraged him from picking out a dress as a gift, saying it was a known fail.

'Men rarely judge their wives' dress size correctly, and there is nothing worse than that. Too big and it's 'You think I'm fat!' Too small and *they* think they're fat! Buy her a beautiful silk evening bag. It covers everything you want.'

This woman knew her stuff. I didn't want to take the dress off. I spun around in it a few times. John stood up and thanked us both for our help and excused himself to look for a silk purse.

I knew I needed to follow him and keep at it. But seeing myself in the dressing-room mirror again made me stop.

'I wish I had somewhere to wear this dress,' I said, drawing the attention of only the saleswoman.

'A dress like that has no business waiting around for a chance to go somewhere.'

Neither do I, I thought as I motioned for her to unzip me. She did. So much for channeling Mata Hari.

'I'll take it when you're done,' she instructed. 'I have to hold it for another customer.'

I knew I'd detected a hidden agenda — *hidden agenda!* I'd gotten so caught up in the dress I'd forgotten I was still on John's trail. I threw on my clothes and caught up with him by the escalator.

'Want some help picking out a purse?' I asked, feeling more like a stalker than a seductress. He nodded. Actually it was more of a shrug, but I went with it.

We headed to the first floor to look at the purses, and he put a lot of thought into his choice. My gut was talking to me very loudly by this point, and I didn't think there was any way this guy was cheating. If I had any doubt, it was obliterated when the salesgirl offered him one of those small free gift cards. He whipped a Hallmark-type anniversary card out of his pocket. On the soft pink envelope he had drawn a big heart. In my experience, these just weren't the actions of a cheater. For the first time in a while, I felt a surge of optimism about the possibility of finding a good man. I couldn't wait to tell Caroline the good news.

16

How to Dress a Broadway Diva

By Her Frustrated Costume Designer
Age: Too old for this nonsense!

'How to dress a Broadway diva' is a question I would have felt confident answering after the thirty-seven productions that have made up my reputable career as a costume designer thus far: eighteen Broadway, twelve Off-Broadway, and seven summer stock. But the current production I am working on, *That Southern Play*, has me doubting it all.

Set in the South, the play has been trumpeted as an homage to the works of Tennessee Williams, most evidently *The Glass Menagerie* and a lesser-known play called *Suddenly Last Summer*. Like *That Southern Play*, they both examine insanity. The insanity in this production, both on and off the stage, involved the lead character, Daphne Beauregard, being played by the Hollywood screen star Jordana Winston.

Being a costume designer for a period piece is usually my favorite kind of work; I

151

enjoy the challenge of creating a past world. *That Southern Play* is set in that small sliver of the sixties before the hippies and the British invaded our culture. When people still dressed for dinner and things like white gloves and ascots were common accessories, especially in the South. As I sketched out my ideas and collected treasures from costume and vintage shops around the city, I felt lucky to be a part of this new production. Just like those unsuspecting proper folk in the early sixties, I had no idea what was coming.

The nightmare began on day two of rehearsals. Day two was the day that the infamous Hollywood leading lady Jordana Winston arrived onstage, or on set, as she mistakenly kept calling it.

It has become common practice of late to feature Hollywood stars on the Broadway stage, and if you ask me, which no one does, it's a travesty. The Tinsel Town effect, as it's called, may boost sales, but it certainly doesn't boost morale, at least not among real Broadway thespians. Prominent stage actors worry that they will disappear from Broadway's future if screen actors continue to scoop up leading roles and Tony Award noms. Some are cast just for their names and aren't even right for the parts. This was especially true in the case of my latest diva, Jordana Winston.

Ms. Winston arrived straight off a mega-million-dollar box office smash, and boy, did she know it. Between her ego and her entourage, it was thought she would need two dressing rooms. This was after her request to airlift a movie trailer onto the ninety-year-old roof of the Brooks Atkinson Theatre was denied. I'm sure the renowned *New York Times* critic Brooks Atkinson, for whom the theater is named, would have had a choice word or two to say about Ms. Jordana Winston. I only wish he could be resurrected for opening night!

Ms. Winston had her own stylist, her own makeup artist, her own trainer/nutritionist, and her own mancubine masquerading as personal manager. (It was quite clear to all what part of her person he managed.) Luckily, all but the last were forbidden by Actors' Equity and sent packing. The diva was furious. She had no idea of the union rules. In fact, I've heard that she has yet even to sign her contract.

She was impossible throughout all her fittings. She kept insisting that she was a smaller size than she was. Her previous stylist must have been letting out her entire wardrobe at the seams, though it's infinitely easier to take in a larger size. She must've been more concerned with the size of Ms. Winston's ego than the size of her ass. I had no patience for such nonsense, and when Ms. Winston realized it she threatened to have me fired. She didn't scare me.

Even though that stylist flew back west in a huff — on a broomstick, no doubt — she still had one opportunity to make my job more difficult. Last week the cast was invited to do a photo shoot for an upcoming *New York* magazine spread on the best new plays of the season. Of course *That Southern Play* was included. The instructions were to dress up, and Ms. Winston's West Coast stylist loaned her a Max Hammer that *WWD* had dubbed the *it* dress of the season. I have to admit it was a good choice. It was very flattering and had not yet reached saturation point in the press. I sent it back to the stylist within a day of the shoot, and unlike most of my dealings with Jordana Winston and her people, this transaction was seamless. Until yesterday, that is, when I was told a reshoot would be necessary because Ms. Winston had gotten her leading man fired. Mine was not the only livelihood she'd been threatening.

Poor Austin Williams. He was an unknown, cast as Ms. Winston's charming, rebellious husband. Yesterday he was let go for no apparent reason. At least that's what the press said. All they knew was that he was to be replaced by his understudy for the run of the show. But the real story was obvious from the first dress rehearsal: the unknown Austin Williams was a star. You felt it the moment he stepped onstage; he owned it the minute he spoke his first line, and as each line left his lips you became more and more glued to him. Glued in such a way that you would find it hard to avert your eyes in case you were to miss one movement, one breath, one perfect utterance in that perfect southern drawl. The problem was, he wasn't meant to be the star. Ms. Winston was. And when put next to this beautiful specimen of theatrical perfection, she was reduced to scenery. Faded right into the background. That is, until she spoke and her painfully inaccurate accent, waxing and waning like a crescent moon, shocked you into paying attention to her again, only making you more grateful to have Mr. Williams there to both save and steal the show. Clearly Ms. Winston was no dummy, and though everyone kept telling her how wonderful she was, she knew that next to Mr. Williams she would not survive.

The reason I knew this? The screaming from her dressing room was so loud that the dressers and I literally locked ourselves in the costume room. It lasted for days. The producers were on edge, the director unhinged, and the other actors took to hanging out in the costume room as well, since it was the farthest from the carnage. I even had Austin's understudy, a sweet kid from Juilliard, gluing sequins. And then yesterday the main producer came asking for him. He looked like he'd just returned from war.

He said, 'Kid, you're on.'

The kid jumped up, knocking over a box of sequins. 'On . . . for rehearsal?' he asked, confused.

'On for the run of the show. The *Playbills* are being reprinted as we speak.'

New York magazine agreed to reshoot the photo on a moment's notice, and I called my very favorite saleswoman in all of Manhattan, Ruthie from Bloomingdale's, to see if she could help me with the dress. She told me she thought she could, and I agreed that I would stop by the store tomorrow.

The next day when I walked in she came out from the back room to greet me with a smile and the Max Hammer. I knew she'd come through. I've known her almost the entire time she's been here. You don't see so many of these tried-and-true New Yorkers anymore, the hardcore no-nonsense type. I always love doing business with Ruthie.

'Here you go!' she said, handing me the dress. 'It's the last small. I nearly lost it to a customer right after I hung up with you yesterday. You may have to steam it out — it's really made the rounds, this dress, seen a lot of action.' She laughed.

'So has the actress who's wearing it, I'm told!'

She laughed harder. I was happy the dress wasn't perfect. I hated being entrusted with a brand-new dress and then returning it in poor shape. I was confident that Jordana Winston would stretch it, stain it, and then leave it in a ball on the floor. Especially since she'd asked to keep it through the opening-night party.

'I'll have it back to you early next week. Is that okay, Ruthie?'

'Absolutely,' she said, adding, 'break a leg, little black dress!'

17

Me and My Beard

By Jeremy Madison, Movie Star

Hank planned to take care of the whole Albert-is-the-love-of-my-life media panic with another staged performance. He wasn't even consulting Albert or me anymore, just barking orders. That night Albert and his boyfriend were to 'bump into' paparazzi outside Nobu 57, where they would explain the entire misunderstanding and emphatically restate that *Jeremy Madison is not gay*. They would both joke about how they wished he were, for the sake of gay men everywhere. Hank felt that the world would believe it coming from two gay men. It would be a perfect Hank Haberman production.

I vowed to do my part for integrity by ensuring that at least the statement 'Jeremy Madison could not be reached for comment' wouldn't be a lie. I planned to be wheels up by four p.m. on my way solo to a private Wi-Fi-free beach without a reporter in sight. I figured I could use some alone time to think

— until Natalie called to check on me, when I decided some Natalie time would be even better. Though I had sworn off rejection, I couldn't resist inviting her to come along. I had fun with her, and she was the perfect distraction from everything I was trying to escape.

'Do you have any time off coming?' I asked.

'I do . . . but I'm supposed to put in for it in advance. Why?'

'I need a vacation. I want to lie on a beach for a few days. Want to come with?' I said, hoping I didn't sound too desperate.

'Mmmm, beach sounds heavenly. When were you thinking?'

'Um . . . now?' I held my breath.

'Ha, I love it. Let me see if Tomás or Ruthie can cover for me. Give me ten minutes.'

'Don't you want to know where we're going?' I asked, laughing at her blind willingness. *Maybe she does like me after all.*

'I don't care — all I need to know is beach. We'll be like Thelma and Louise! Maybe we'll even pick up Brad Pitt somewhere along the way!'

It was like a one-two punch: she saw me as her gal pal, *and* she wanted Brad Pitt. 'Okay, call me back,' I somehow recovered enough to say.

My BFF Natalie and I met at Teterboro at four to board a private plane. She was so excited when she saw me that she leaped into my arms and wrapped her legs around my waist. She loved the private plane — her first time. She loved that the destination was a surprise. And at the first sight of the breath-taking coastline of Turks and Caicos her eyes almost popped out of her head. She thanked me more on that plane ride and on the way to the resort than my ex had in our entire relationship. I made a mental note to stop comparing her to my ex and start comparing her to Mitchell Grabow, my best friend at Camp Olympus.

When we went to check in I asked for two different casitas, one for each of us.

Natalie quickly jumped in: 'We're not staying in the same room?' *She likes me?*

'I just thought, well, what if your Brad Pitt is roaming around? You need to have a place to take him.'

She laughed. 'If either of us finds our Brad Pitt, we can just go to his room!'

What the hell was she talking about? What would I want with Brad Pitt? Although actually I would love to meet Brad Pitt. He made the transition from twentysomething heartthrob to real grownup actor perfectly. She knows me better in a few weeks than my fiancée did after a year.

She shook my shoulder and said pretty seriously, 'Jeremy, I want to spend every minute with you. I haven't felt this close to anyone this quickly since Lisa Rogell moved next door in the sixth grade!'

. . . likes me the way she liked Lisa Rogell.

'One casita, please.' For me and my bestie.

Our houseboy drove us to our room in a golf cart and showed us everything we would need to know. The place was perfect — simple but luxuriously comfortable. The bedroom was a glass-walled room jutting out onto the rocks overlooking the ocean. It was very minimalist. Just a sumptuous white king-sized bed, two walk-in closets, and a bathroom fit for a king.

Within minutes Natalie was quite minimalist herself, in her string bikini, her beautiful smile, and a sheer beaded sarong. It wasn't just her beauty that attracted me, the lines of her face and curves of her body; it was her whole being. Her aura. She was somehow both engaging and unobtainable. I threw on a suit and a T-shirt and we headed down to the beach.

Once we were there, a cabana boy approached to set us up. Natalie pointed to a secluded sunbed near the ocean and asked if it was available.

'For you, of course,' he answered.

'Is that okay with you?' she asked me.

'Whatever makes you happy,' I answered. She smiled. My ex would have turned that into a twenty-minute argument about me not clearly stating my needs or giving her what she wanted just to win points. She was always talking about points for her side and points for my side. I was doing it again, comparing Natalie to my ex. I tried thinking of her as Mitch Grabow, but the glow of her skin was making it really difficult.

The cabana boy set us up with towels and ice water and Natalie ordered us two piña coladas. She lay down right next to me. Not touching me, but so close that her legs would occasionally brush up against mine. She sat up. 'Are you bored?' I wasn't. I was happy just lying there wondering when her leg was going to brush up against mine again. She rooted around in her bag and pulled out the two scripts I was supposed to read — I had charged her with making me — and sunscreen. 'We should definitely put this on now,' she said, gesturing for me to turn over onto my stomach. She proceeded to put sunscreen on my back, then asked that I return the favor. *Mitch Grabow, Mitch Grabow*, I thought, but as I rubbed the soft white cream over her shoulders, I knew I was a goner. When I reached the two dimples that sat like the gates to Disney World on the top of her bum, I knew I couldn't take any more. 'All done!' I said, trying not to sound as turned on as I was.

'Which script do you want to read first?' she asked, holding one up on either side of her happy face.

'Neither!' I laughed.

'Come on, I'll read it to you. I'll even do the voices.' This was exactly what I needed to take my mind off Hank and Albert and the press.

'Here.' I tapped on the lighter one. It was a romantic comedy. Hank thought that after my last two action films I should do something sexy and funny and overtly heterosexual. This film was shooting next month, and they were looking to replace the lead at the last minute — rumor was that the original lead had entered rehab. Hank was begging me to take it. Maybe a happy ending onscreen would rub off on my personal life.

She began.

'Fade In. EXT.' She stopped, the cutest frown wrinkling her forehead. 'What's EXT?' she asked.

I went over the notations with her. 'EXT means exterior — it means the scene is outside.' I flipped a few pages in and pointed.

'INT means interior — the scene is inside. Sometimes it says INT/EXT, which would be looking inside from outside, like through a window. Get it?'

'Yes. This is so cool!'

'For you maybe. You know how many scripts I have to read before I find the right one? Or more often the wrong one.'

'Well, I'm gonna read this one, so keep explaining,' she instructed.

'Okay. It's pretty simple. After that we have the scene description in all caps, under that the action, and then the dialogue. The dialogue is always written under the characters' names.' I handed the script back to her. 'Here, try it.' It was great having it read to me so I could just lie in the sun and listen and try to picture it.

She sat up and began.

'Exterior. Snowy day, ski resort, Vermont. Nancy Straub waits with bated breath at the foot of the mountain. She anxiously looks at her watch. She stares up the mountain again and — *Oh my god, look by the tiki bar, it's Flip's fiancée.*'

I opened my eyes. 'What? Let me see that,' I said, reaching for the script. 'A tiki bar in a Vermont ski resort? This already makes no sense. Let's read the other one.' I took the script from Natalie's shaking hands.

Her eyes were teary. 'It's not in the script. It's real. It's Flip's fiancée. I recognize her from the wedding announcement and the many Google and Facebook searches I did on her. This must be their honeymoon. Oh my god, and there's Flip! He saw us! They're coming this way!'

She looked heartbroken. I couldn't take it — I'd whisked us both away to escape, and I'd brought her face-to-face with the one thing she most wanted to forget about. It was like one of those ridiculous coincidence scenes in a romantic comedy. Only in the rom-com the writer would have saved the day with some huge romantic gesture. So I thought, *What would Nora Epbron have me do?* I scooped Natalie up in my arms and carried her into the calm blue ocean. She laughed nervously and wrapped her hands around my neck as I dunked us both up to our waists. She was playacting. I was sure her motivation was to put on a show for Flip, while I ceased acting the minute she wrapped her arms around my neck. I had such strong feelings for this girl. I could see Flip heading toward us, nonplussed by the little scene we were creating. He seemed determined.

Natalie whispered, 'Are they still coming our way?'

She actually looked scared. 'I got this!' I

responded, and kissed her. At first gently on the lips but then passionately and with everything I had. I don't know if it was from vengeance or passion, but she responded equally, and anyone within view, including Flip and his new wife, got quite a show. Both of us kept going, though probably for different reasons. I kept going because I was enjoying it immensely; I imagined she kept going because she was just plain scared of what would happen when we pulled apart. We continued until the famous — and surprisingly short — Flip Roberts called out to us.

'Natalie? Is that you?' he shouted from the shore, his somewhat attractive wife by his side. Nothing was stopping this guy.

She gave me a shrug as if to say, 'We can't stay in this ocean forever.'

I carried her back out and placed her right by my side in the sand. She straightened herself out and asked, as if she'd been acting all her life, 'Oh my, Flip. What are you doing here?'

'I thought that was you.' He stumbled on his words.

'We're on our honeymoon!' the somewhat attractive wife responded with a sting. And then it happened. We both saw it. She recognized me. She nudged Flip three times and then outright kicked him. Natalie tried to fight the smirk that formed on her lips but finally lost to a full-on smile when the wife asked straight out, 'Are you Jeremy Madison?'

I smiled my best movie-star smile and answered, 'Not this weekend. This weekend I'm just Natalie Canaras's boyfriend, so please, please don't spread it around that you've seen us. We came here to escape the press.' Flip looked like he wanted to die.

His wife was pretty, I guess, in an uptight kind of way, but nothing compared to Natalie. There is no way she could have Natalie's spirit, or sweetness, or soul — not possible. Though I still couldn't figure out how Natalie had ever been attracted to this guy, I wanted her to be happy, and if sticking it to Flip made her happy, then I would lay it on thick. Natalie had yet to speak, the wife yet to shut up.

'Maybe we can all have dinner together one night,' she said eagerly. I looked to Nat for the answer. She smiled yes but her eyes screamed no. I wrapped my arms around her.

'I'm sorry,' I said, 'but we'll be eating all our meals back at our casita. It's a short stay and I want her all to myself.' I tickled her a bit. She laughed. Flip died. His bride looked on with envy — not because I was a movie star, I thought, but because what makes a woman feel better than a man saying he wants her all to himself? I added, a bit cruelly to Flip, 'You must understand that.' Flip made a noise halfway between a cough and a splutter as he took his wife's hand purposefully.

'Goodbye — enjoy,' he said, turning and marching away across the sand.

'You too,' Natalie called after them, barely suppressing a giggle.

If she could have jumped up and down in the sand fist-pumping with complete abandon, I think she would have. Instead she curled up next to me on the sunbed and leaned against my chest. 'Jeremy,' she said, 'you are the finest actor I've ever seen, and I will never, ever forget what you just did for me. Ever.' She kissed me quickly on the lips. The way you kiss a puppy.

The next few days were spent mostly in and in front of our casita in our private pool. This break was exactly what I needed — peaceful, with no chance of being recognized, plus we read both scripts and I was seriously considering doing the romantic comedy set in Vermont. Natalie was also happy to hole up. Though she liked to be around people, she wanted to avoid seeing Flip again. She didn't want to ruin the perfect bump-into. Apparently this was a thing; I'd never even considered it, but girls spend a lot of time obsessing over it. When will they bump into their ex-boyfriends? Will they look good or will they be walking home from the gym on the hottest day of the year? And it has to be unplanned to qualify as a true bump-into. It can't be, let's say, at a wedding, where you have the heads-up and know to look your absolute best. Apparently bumping into your ex while frolicking in the waves with an A-list movie star and looking great in a bikini was like hitting the trifecta of bump-intos.

At night she would sleep in the almost nude, on her stomach, and she would always fall asleep before me. I would watch her. Not in a creepy way, I swear. Her suntanned body and her peaceful face and her tousled hair — it was like looking at a sunset. I couldn't help but watch her until my eyes got tired and shut as well. Two more nights and I would have to fall asleep to Jimmy Fallon again. I used to think that was just fine.

She was obsessed with the great service at the hotel. She had been so pleased to learn that whenever you threw something into the little hamper in our room, it magically appeared clean and folded on our bed a few hours later. She didn't take anything for granted and was grateful for everything. It made me realize how much I needed that in my life. On our last night we ordered in lobsters and champagne, and on account of everything being clean and dry and packed up, Natalie convinced me to go skinny-dipping. I know you're thinking I probably didn't need that much convincing, but I didn't think I'd be able to make it through. I'd somewhat resigned myself to being platonic, and had gotten used to keeping a safe distance. I wasn't sure I'd be able to stop myself from kissing her if we were naked in the water together. But she really wanted to go, and I couldn't say no to her.

I was right — I wasn't able to make it through. By the third time she brushed by me and rose above the water looking like a Greek goddess of the sea, I pulled her toward me and kissed her. It lasted a few minutes, and I don't think I'd ever wanted anyone so badly or waited so long to act on it. I broke away.

'Should we go inside to continue this?' I asked, barely audible.

'I don't think we should continue, Jeremy,' she responded, completely audible.

'Why?' I asked, a little surprised.

'Why?' she responded, and seemed even more surprised. My desire began to wane. I didn't know what her deal was, but I was beginning to feel toyed with.

'Yes, why? Why are you all gaga over that

idiot who can't see past his Ivy League rulebook and for me you feel nothing?' I had said it. I don't remember ever leaving myself so vulnerable in my life. She stopped for a moment to think. I felt very naked, and I think she did too as she crossed her arms over her breasts as she spoke.

'Jeremy, I've just had my heart broken, and I didn't like it. In fact I pretty much hated it, and I don't want to go through that again, at least not so — '

I interrupted her. 'Natalie, I'm absolutely crazy about you, everything about you. Every minute with you leaves me wanting more. I promise I will not hurt you,' I pleaded.

'You say that now, Jeremy, and I'm sure you believe it, but down deep inside you like men, and I know that with the moonlight and the nakedness and all this pretending to be a couple you temporarily found me attractive, but I think you're just caught up in the moment.'

'*Hold on!*' I shouted. 'What the hell are you talking about? I'm not gay.'

Her face turned ashen. She backed away from me and ran to get a towel. I ran after her. I was confused, but she just seemed angry. She was pacing around the room throwing her last few belongings in her suitcase. Finally she stopped.

'How could you?' she asked.

'How could I what?' I responded.

'How could you have lied to me like that? And for so long. You slept in my bed . . . and you brought me here and shared a room with me. I was naked in front of you!'

'I'm sorry . . . I thought you were just a free spirit — it's one of the things I like about you!'

'Really?' She seethed. 'Well, I'm not. I'm not a free spirit! I'm a prude! I'm only a free spirit in front of my girlfriends! Thelma and Louise, remember?'

'I never told you I was gay!' I said, losing my temper a bit.

'You never told me you weren't!' she shouted, losing hers a lot.

She yelled at me without giving me the chance to defend myself. I kept thinking it would end up okay, but she was possibly the most stubborn person I'd ever met, and the night ended with her sleeping, I kid you not, in the bathtub fit for a king, with all the bedding and most of the pillows. The next day I didn't know what to say and she seemed to have said everything she felt, so we rode home on the private plane in silence. Except for one parting sentence — hers.

'Goodbye, Jeremy. I liked you better when you were gay.'

She took her own cab from Teterboro. In the limo home I consoled myself with one reassuring fact: although now she didn't like me in *that* way or in any way whatsoever, at least before she hadn't liked me in *that* way because I was gay.

18

Love in the Afternoon

By Felicia (aka Arthur Winters' Executive Assistant)

He got me there on the pretext of needing a file for a client. The whole way over I secretly thought he'd remembered I had said the Carlyle was on my bucket list. Of course I'd said it picturing us listening to Sutton Foster at the Café, not in a tryst in a suite upstairs. Looks like I may have to write myself a new list!

I went to the front desk as instructed and asked for Mr. Winters.

The concierge said there was a note for me. 'Suite 402' was written in the most familiar handwriting I knew, with a little heart drawn on the bottom of the card. That part was new to me. I pressed the fourth-floor button six times, but it didn't make the elevator go any faster.

Within seconds of entering the room I was naked between what felt like million-thread-count sheets. Arthur kissed me and then pushed back to the foot of the bed. This scene, of a woman being pleasured by a man and responding with reckless abandon, is being played out in the movies and on television more frequently lately. It must have something to do with the resurgence of the feminist movement. I thanked those young feminists in my head for making me slightly more comfortable with it, but still I tensed up. It's the reckless abandon that I've never been able to get a handle on. I just never felt comfortable enough with someone to let him do that. The few times someone had tried, I'd literally said, 'No, thank you.' No, thank you, like I was turning down dessert.

Arthur must have sensed something because he returned to face me. He kissed me on the mouth. 'What's the matter?' He kissed me again.

'Nothing,' I said, but I could hear the nervousness in my voice.

He must have heard it too. He smiled and looked into my eyes. 'C'mon. It's me,' he said before heading down my body again. And somehow then I got lost in it.

An hour later, as I watched him sleep, I realized with a sinking heart that I would probably have to leave him. This was getting serious, for me at least. And he had yet to officially break it off with Sherri, although he promised he would. He opened his eyes.

'Arthur,' I said, very seriously, 'tomorrow afternoon I'm going to meet with a headhunter.'

He laughed. 'That's a setup for a sex joke if I ever heard one.'

'I'm serious, Arthur. I shouldn't be working for you anymore.' I sighed. 'Partners shouldn't break the rules.'

He looked sad. 'If you don't work for me, then I won't see you every day. I don't think I could bear it.'

Now I laughed. 'You haven't even broken up with Sherri yet. She called three times yesterday.'

'I know. She's calling so often because I haven't seen her.' He sighed heavily. 'I'm just trying to find the right time. She's not the strongest. I'm scared of hurting her.' I looked at him and rolled my eyes.

'You're right. I'll do it this weekend. You go to the headhunter, and by next week we will no longer have to skulk around.'

I felt completely content. Being with Arthur this way felt both so new and so old at the same time.

He laughed. 'I'm going to miss the skulking, though. This has been my only skulking experience, and I have to admit, it's sort of fun.'

I laughed too. 'It is fun. We still have a little skulking time left. I'm sure I won't get a job right away.'

'That's true.' He peeked under the covers and added, 'I bet a lot of that depends on my recommendation.' And we were at it again.

19

Opening Night

By the Diva's Mancubine
Age: Same as the diva's
(if I told you, I'd have to kill you)

I knew every line by heart. Every stage
direction and scene description as well. I had
rehearsed every part over and over, except of
course for Jordana's. I had to concentrate
hard not to move my lips along with the
performance.

ACT ONE

(The curtain rises on DAPHNE BEAURE-
GARD in bed. It's a hot August day
in Georgia, around eleven o'clock
on a Sunday morning. LUCINDA,
the maid, enters with a tray of iced tea
and biscuits. She puts down the tray
and draws the curtains. Daphne, still
wearing her eye mask, stirs and reaches
to her husband's side of the bed.
It's empty.)

178

DAPHNE Reggie is up bright and early, I see.
LUCINDA It's almost noon, Mrs. Beauregard.
DAPHNE A girl needs her beauty sleep, Lucinda.

Lucinda fixes the curtains across the room.

LUCINDA Maybe you could use a few more hours.
DAPHNE What was that, Lucinda?
LUCINDA I said, Mr. Beauregard has been out riding for hours.
DAPHNE We have cocktails at the Whitmans' tonight. I want to wear that darling dress I bought last week in Atlanta. They said Jackie Kennedy has the same one. Lay out my diamonds and my pearls — I'll start dressing at five. Oh, which shoes shall I wear? Better make it four-thirty. I have quite a few decisions to make.
LUCINDA As you wish, Mrs. Beauregard.
DAPHNE And for the hundredth time, Lucinda, you need not call me Mrs. Beauregard.
LUCINDA Sorry, ma'am.
DAPHNE Much better. Tomorrow I'll be lunching in town. Please spend that time

179

dusting off my snow-globe collection. And make sure it's when Rose is napping. I don't want her touching them.

LUCINDA I know that, Mrs. Beauregard.

DAPHNE For the love of sweet Jesus, please call me ma'am.

At that point I stopped running the lines in my head. I was distracted by the man next to me. He had a small notebook. Probably a critic. He wrote down three words. I tried to read out of the corner of my eye.

Over her head.

Over her head. Oh boy. Could he be talking about the maid? For the love of sweet Jesus, please let him be talking about the maid. Maybe he was from *Newsday*. We could survive a bad review from *Newsday*. As long as it wasn't the *Times*. Jesus — seven lines in and he already thinks she's in over her head. And she hasn't even slipped out of her southern accent yet. That usually doesn't happen till Act Two.

Daphne's husband entered the scene. His disdain for Daphne was palpable. As was the critic's disdain for Jordana. He wrote a word I'd hoped not to see.

Ambitious.

You may think of this word as complimentary. I knew it wasn't. I pictured his review.

Ms. Winston might have chosen a less ambitious role for her Broadway debut. One that didn't have her accent stray farther south of her native Los Angeles than, let's say, Pasadena.

Onstage, Reggie Beauregard took hold of Daphne's most precious snow globe — an antique replica of Niagara Falls — and threw it to the ground.

Daphne shrieks.

DAPHNE Not the Niagara Falls! You know that belonged to Mama!
REGINALD Well, now it belongs to no one. And if you don't stop meddling in my business, you will belong to no one as well.

Reginald exits stage right. Daphne throws herself onto the bed and sobs.

Curtain down. End of Act One

The critic and his companion hurried to the bar as soon as the lights came on for intermission. I sidled up next to them, ordered a martini, and searched Web images of New York theater critics on my phone. I nearly choked on my olive. The man standing next to me was none other than Brad Bentley, chief drama critic for the *New York Times*. This is a total nightmare.

'She is way too old for that part. The guy who plays Reginald could be her son,' said his crony. Bentley agreed as he ordered another scotch. Maybe he would sleep through the second act. What was I going to do? A bad review in the *Times* would devastate her. Too old for the part? I could not imagine the hell and Botox a remark like that would bring about.

He spoke to his friend. 'At least you can leave. I have to stay for the second act!' His friend dismissed the suggestion, but I took it.

I ran from the theater as if it were on fire and hailed a cab. You may wonder what I see in this narcissistic prima donna beyond a meal ticket, but I love her. I do. There's something underneath the drama, underneath the ego, that speaks to me. We understand each other. And I'm her person. It's better being her person than being the person I am without her — an out-of-work actor who hasn't been cast in anything since *Titanic*, when my character's name was First to Drown. Well, I wasn't going to drown today. Today I was going to jump ship, and I was going to take my darling egomaniac leading lady with me.

I made all the necessary arrangements in the car back to the hotel. The second act was only fifty minutes long, so I had to multitask. The three-hour time difference between New York and L.A. helped. I called Jordana's assistant back home and had her arrange first-class tickets for the midnight flight to Paris and a suite at the Plaza Athénée. At three a.m., when the reviews came out, we would be sound asleep somewhere over the Atlantic. Thank god and her agent that she never signed that contract. I ran up to our suite, threw some essentials and half her wardrobe in my black wheelie bag, grabbed our passports, and was back in my seat before the finale.

In my absence Daphne and Reggie had returned from the Whitmans' dinner party, where Daphne had accused Reggie of groping the Whitmans' maid in the pantry. As payback he'd smashed every last one of her snow globes. This drove her mad, and the play wrapped up with Jordana wrapped up in a straitjacket, being taken away to an asylum.

The curtain dropped. People clapped, mostly I think because it was over, and I hurried backstage during the curtain call to wait for her in her dressing room. She came bursting in, full of exuberance and hope. Actually, it wasn't hope — she was completely certain she'd been fabulous.

'Was I fabulous, darling? Tell me!' It was definitely a 'Tell me!' not a 'Tell me?' Already down to just her slip, she reached for the little black dress she was to wear to the opening-night party. She couldn't wait to take in all the accolades she was sure would be forthcoming.

I broke it to her gently. I knew it would hurt less coming from me. I'm her person; this is what I do.

'I thought you were fabulous, baby, really I did, but I sat next to Brad Bentley, you know, the critic from the *Times* — '

She interrupted me; her exuberance had turned to irritation. 'Of course I know who Brad Bentley is. I wasn't born yesterday!'

'Well, he seems to have noticed that. And I'm pretty sure that he's writing that you're in over your head. I'm sorry.'

She sat down and breathed. She could be pretty clear-headed when it came to her own damage control. 'The reviews will be out at three a.m., right?'

I nodded.

'Did you see anything else?'

'He wrote the word *ambitious*,' I said, in as humane a whisper as I could.

She grimaced. She knew that word was lethal. 'We need to be as far from here as possible when that review comes out!'

'How's Paris?' I pulled out the wheelie bag I'd stashed before sneaking back to my seat and told her that everything was arranged. We went out the front of the theater to avoid the crowds that would be waiting by the stage door and jumped into a waiting car. She stripped off the little black dress that had been so full of promise when it had arrived, shoved it in the luggage, and threw on the disguise I had brought her: a Juicy Couture tracksuit and a dark brown wig.

'The show must go on!' she proclaimed grandly. 'Without me!'

'JFK Airport,' I said to the driver as I marveled at her resilience.

20

The Juicy Couture
Tracksuit vs. the Burqa

By Medina Karim, Shireen's Levelheaded
Sister Age: 16

I was used to the stares, but somehow my sister wasn't. Even though she was two years older than me — you'd think that's two more years to get used to it. Our entire trip to New York City was narrated by her complaining about the stares. Even just now, while my sister was complaining about it, I noticed a woman in an obvious wig and an ugly Juicy Couture tracksuit staring at us.

You may think it odd that I am familiar with Juicy Couture, but I know of the latest fashions as well as the outdated ones. You may think it odd because I am wearing a burqa. So is my sister. So is my mother. But my sister reads all the latest French fashion magazines. We live in Paris. In her dreams she lives in a fantasy world where people stare at her because she is beautifully dressed from head to toe in the latest Chanel or Dolce &

Gabbana, not because she is robed from head to toe in her religion. Her eyes often well up in response to the reactions of strangers. I believe those tears are due to her own disappointment that she is not a Westerner or, even more ridiculous, a Western model on the pages of a fashion magazine. I fan through the magazines when she is finished with them, but I do not live in a fantasyland and I'm honored to wear a burqa. I wish she would seek refuge with Allah and give up these thoughts.

Suddenly my sister, Shireen, noticed the Juicy Couture woman as well. I wondered what took her this long. 'Look, over there, that woman in the out-of-style tracksuit is staring at us. We should stare at her in that putrid outfit! She can wear anything she wants and that's what she chooses?' The woman made matters worse by whispering something to the man next to her, doing a sort of half point in our direction. A quick poke for his attention, then a flick of the wrist to direct him to look at the circus act: Muslim women dressed in full burqas in the Western world.

'What do you think she's saying about us?' Shireen asked me.

I softened it, as I always did. 'It's hot in here. Maybe she's saying, see those girls with the pretty eyes — they must be hot.'

'I am hot,' Shireen responded, even more annoyed at realizing it. We both looked over at our younger brother in his New York Yankees T-shirt. This infuriated her more — him wearing that T-shirt and us cloaked in our religion. She did not feel the strong bond that I did to our mother and her mother before her in our native Saudi Arabia. My mother knew this, to some extent. Last year she even bought Shireen a special burqa made of crepe, with black velvet trim. Shireen told me the velvet made her cry more. It was like a taste of something that left her wanting.

She interrupted my thoughts. 'Dalia was all wrong about New York, all wrong,' she complained. Dalia is our cousin who spent last summer in New York. She went on and on about how Manhattan was different from Paris, how people didn't stare so much. How in New York you could walk down the street with a camel and no one would stare at you. She was right in that New York is a melting pot. America in general is much more of a melting pot than anywhere in Europe, I think. Europe has a lot of different nationalities in each country, of course, but they never really seem to melt together. You can move to Germany, but you never really become a German. The same is very true of France, and I have been living there since the age of two. In America anyone can become a true American. What Dalia was wrong about was the staring. There are people in New York who seem content to spend their whole day perched on benches staring at other people. It even has a name: people-watching. It's like bird-watching but without the binoculars. Still, it didn't bother me.

Shireen decided she was going to take down the Juicy Couture starer with just her eyes. She'd had enough. She stood and walked toward Juicy and the guy she was with and gave them a good, long, obvious stare back. It actually worked. They ran off to a corner and sat with magazines plastered in front of their faces until our flight was called. We laughed so hard that it drew my father's attention, which was not a good thing. They called for our flight to board at just the right time.

Once on the plane, Shireen looked sad again. I didn't have to ask her why. She would be married in two weeks' time, and the trip to New York, which she had thought would satisfy her yearning to explore, had done nothing for her. We had barely been allowed out of our father's sight; thinking it would be any other way had been just a silly dream of hers. She would be married in two weeks to a man she barely knew and did not love. I know she had dreamed of things that have never even entered my mind. Dreams of dressing in the clothing on the pages of the magazines and attracting a man — even though those dreams defy the exact reason that we wear a burqa: to protect us from the lustful gaze of men. Shireen *yearned* for the lustful gaze of men. She dreamed of kissing a man. Not her husband, just any man. It is a sin to kiss anything with the intention of lust, anything, even a rock. I didn't envy her dreams. They brought her only dissatisfaction with life.

21

Indiscretion at
the Ostrich Detective Agency

By Andie Rand, Private Detective

It had been two weeks since my interaction with John Westmont, but I was still thinking about it like it was yesterday. I had nearly skipped the whole way home from Bloomingdale's. I mean not really skipped, but there was an extra bounce in my step. I was anticipating my phone call with Caroline and the relief that she would feel when I told her the good news. I thought about what I would say. *He's a keeper, Caroline! You got one of the good ones!* A little unprofessional, I thought. But it was such a rarity for me to have this kind of storybook ending. In fact, it's only happened twice in the three years I've been in the business. When one spouse thinks the other is cheating, they're most often right. I'm not talking about the ordinary paranoia people sometimes feel in a marriage, I'm talking about enough paranoia to cause you to seek professional help. But

191

the Westmonts had restored my faith in the sanctity of marriage. At least for the half hour it took me to not really skip home.

I called Caroline's cell and left her a message asking her to call me back. She called back within minutes. My cheerful 'Hello, Caroline!' was met with a whisper from the other end.

'Why are you whispering?' I whispered in return.

'Because I'm hiding in a closet,' she said, adding, 'John is right outside.'

'Right outside?'

He had said he was meeting her at Le Cirque straight from Bloomingdale's. My heart sank. Had he put one over on me? It couldn't be. Oh my god, I bet the present wasn't even for Caroline. I felt sick.

'Yes,' she said quietly, 'I've had to spend the whole afternoon with him! I'm hoping you have enough dirt for me to cancel our dinner plans in a fitful rage and at least save my evening!'

'You spent the whole afternoon with your husband, John Westmont?' I said incredulously.

'Yes, and every minute with him leaves me feeling more and more demoralized. I can't take much more of this. Please tell me you know something.'

'I know that you're lying to me. Though

I'm not sure why.'

'What are you talking about? What part am I lying about?'

'It can be so hard to tell once you start, can't it? You tell me. Go through all your lies and throw one out at me. Let's see if it sticks.'

My question was met with silence, and my anger boiled over.

'*I* spent the afternoon with your husband,' I said, breaking the silence. 'At Bloomingdale's, helping him pick out an anniversary present for *you*. Let's start with that. Why are you lying to me about that?'

She laughed. *Laughed*. As if her response was going to humor me.

'All right, you caught me. I should have just been straight with you to begin with, but I didn't know if you'd take the case and get me what I needed if you knew the truth. I'm the one having the affair, not John.'

I couldn't even find the words to express how betrayed I felt. Her swollen eyes and monumental lies were all just an act to get me to take on her case. And it didn't help that John was such a nice man. I was furious. I hadn't been lied to like that — to my face and so cavalierly — since Derek, and it really struck a nerve. She continued without missing a beat.

'This is getting tiresome, and it's clearly

not working. We're going to need to do things differently. I knew there was a chance that there'd be nothing to get on John, the patron saint of husbands. I was hoping he'd do something that looked at least halfway suspicious, but he's too boring even for that. It's okay — I have a backup plan.'

She went on about her plan and I listened quietly as my mind reeled. I could have just said, *I'm not interested in your plan, you lying cheat, and you are no longer my client*, but I waited — partly out of curiosity, partly because the extent of her duplicity was slow to sink in.

Her plan was quite elaborate. I was to make another appointment with the masseuse and plant evidence, including a naked picture of John, when I was left alone to disrobe. She would come in later that day to confront her and find said evidence.

At that point I stopped her. I told her that it would never work and that I don't plant evidence, and I fired her as a client. It actually might have worked, but obviously it was criminal and immoral and I wanted no part of it. I spent the rest of that night wallowing in my Cabernet and thinking of poor John with the elegant black silk evening bag and the pink envelope with the heart on it.

Weeks later I was still thinking about him. I was having one of those days when you find a reason to cry in every song you hear. It was an off weekend with my kids, and while you may think that sounds free and liberating I often find it sad, lonely, and depressing. If only the most unconditional love in my life, my dog, Franny, could stay with me, I wouldn't feel as deserted and would have a solid reason to get out of the house. But Franny was included in the visitation agreement. *Better for the kids*, he said. All of a sudden he was concerned with what's better for the kids. The hypocrisy . . .

Even though this is Manhattan and there are a hundred things to do on any given day, I was sitting in my office feeling melancholy. So I decided to check in on what John Westmont was up to. I'd like to say it was the first time I had done this, but I'd be lying. At first I just did it to see whether Caroline had removed the tracker from John's phone, but she hadn't even bothered. Then I just found myself wondering what he was doing. It was bizarre behavior, I admit, but I'd been rather bored lately. He seemed to be moving quickly down Madison Avenue. Realizing with a jolt that what I was doing was no better than common stalking, I exited from the program and vowed not to check again. And I took it one step further. Caroline had set it up so I'd be copied on all John's incoming e-mails. Since she seemed to have no intention of deactivating that either, I decided I would run a search and mark all of them as spam so they would all be redirected into my junk folder from now on. Out of sight, out of mind.

As I started the search, a new e-mail came in for him from the Apple store at Grand Central. I read it. I shouldn't have, but I thought, *It's not personal, it's just the Apple store.*

We've reserved your spot in line at the Genius Bar and will be ready for you soon. You'll get a reminder when it's almost your turn.

From his location on the tracker I realized he must be going to the one in Grand Central Terminal. *He'll be there forever,* I thought. I realized a little too eagerly that I actually did need to go to the Apple Store. And it was the perfect errand for an unplanned day. We were down to one laptop cord in our house and it was causing lots of bickering. It never ceases to amaze me that they can make two-and-a-half-pound devices that carry all your photos, music, movies, work, and the entire Internet but can't make cords that last as long as their computers. I put on my coat and was out the door before you could say 'totally inappropriate.'

As I noticed the Fifth Avenue Apple Store out the window of my cab, heading a whole seventeen blocks and three avenues out of the way to the Apple Store that I hoped John was at, I couldn't help but giggle. I was excited to see him, and the spying element made it more fun — for the time being, at least. I promised myself that if I saw him I wouldn't approach him first. I would let him find me. As if that little deal with myself would magically turn this unethical planned encounter into a real chance meeting.

I checked my (his) e-mail again. There was another.

We'll be ready for you shortly. Please make your way to the Apple store.

It was almost too easy. I often thought about how people in my profession did this before modern technology. Like the detectives who inspired fictional sleuths like Sherlock Holmes and Philip Marlowe. It was a whole different world. My girls had been obsessed with Nancy Drew lately; I like to think that had something to do with what their mom did for a living. I bought them a

197

complete hardcover set of the originals. I began thinking up titles for modern Nancy Drew books: *The Secret Hidden Web Portal*, *The Mystery of the Facebook Group*. My cab pulled over to the curb.

Upon entering the great hall at Grand Central I was, as always, awestruck by its beauty. I've never been a commuter, but I couldn't imagine traveling to and from this place to be a routine worth complaining about. There is something romantic about train travel to begin with, but add in the grandeur and history of Grand Central station and it is downright enchanting: the constellation-covered ceilings, all the times visitors and natives alike have uttered the phrase 'Meet me under the clock at Grand Central,' the majesty of its marble columns and arches. I could stare at the great hall for hours, but I had to move on. I had a mission. I headed to the store as his next Apple e-mail arrived.

Thanks for waiting. We're now ready for you. Please check in with a specialist.

I walked into the narrow store just as John Westmont was being escorted to his seat at the Genius Bar for his appointment. I decided to put myself directly in his line of vision but vowed not to make the first move. I perused the power cords and chose two, pretending to be absorbed in the task. I approached the technician to John's right, who was gently breaking some bad computer news to a woman who looked like she was going to cry. I think they both welcomed the interruption.

'Excuse me, can you please tell me which of these goes with the MacBook Air? I have the thirteen-inch,' I added, purposely not saying the year in case I needed more time to be noticed.

'Which year?' the technician responded, as I knew he would.

'Two thousand fourteen,' I said, which he followed with a tap on the box in my right hand.

'Don't I know you?' asked John Westmont, tapping my left. I looked at him with what I hoped was a quizzical expression.

'You're the lady from Bloomingdale's, right?' He looked at his feet to hide the flush in his cheeks. 'I never got your name.'

I smiled to ease his embarrassment. 'I never gave it to you. I'm Andie.'

'Just Andie?'

'That's right,' I said coyly.

'Okay, then,' he replied, reaching out his hand. 'I'm just John.'

As I took his hand to shake it I felt a little jolt, and it wasn't coming from the power cords. 'How did your wife like the bag?'

'She exchanged it, I think. Well, she said she was going to . . . ' He paused, then said gently, 'I thought it was a great choice though, really. Thank you.'

I smiled, feeling a little regret. Now that my plan was working it felt like a really bad idea. *Just what this man needs is another woman lying to him. I'll say 'Nice seeing you again' and leave,* I thought. This couldn't go anywhere worth going.

'How long is your wait?' he asked.

'Oh, I'm just here for the new cord,' I said.

'That's good.' He smiled. 'From the way my computer's acting, I'm guessing I'll have a bit of time to kill.'

'You're not going to leave it and come back?' I asked, wanting him to say yes but also wanting him to say no.

'Actually, I'm going to do something I've always wanted to — take the walking tour of Grand Central.'

I lit up. I couldn't help it. I had always wanted to take the tour of Grand Central too. I used to ask Derek all the time, but he thought it was too touristy. And then the last few years I hadn't had anyone to go with. It definitely seemed like the kind of thing that was better to do with someone.

'I've always wanted to do that!' I blurted out.

His Genius guy arrived just in time with an introduction and the standard 'What seems to be the problem today?'

I saw this as my chance to get away — I really needed to just leave this man alone — so I reined in my enthusiasm and said in a much calmer tone, 'Good luck. Nice seeing you again.'

As I turned to leave he gently grabbed my forearm. 'Wait — please,' and to the technician, 'The wheel is spinning all the time, and the last time this happened you had to hold it hostage for three hours.' He turned his laptop to face the technician, who took a look, pressed a few buttons, asked John to insert a password, and then voilà.

'Come back at four and it'll be good as new, or close to it.'

'Great, thank you!' John stood and faced me.

'Come with me — you should come,' he said sweetly.

I would love to, I thought as I declined.

'It starts in an hour. We can have lunch at the Oyster Bar first. Go on, say yes.'

I had never done that either, but had always wanted to. I thought about the afternoon that awaited me if I said no. I would leave here, jump on the subway, and spend the rest of my day lying on the couch with my dear friends Don and Betty Draper. Lucky for me, my divorce coincided with the advent of binge television-watching. Now you could justify a lazy day spent in front of the TV watching *Mad Men* as an exercise in staying culturally relevant.

Or I could just say yes. I say it every morning when the man at the corner deli asks if I want milk in my coffee. I stopped making a whole pot after the divorce. It seemed wasteful.

'Yes,' I said.

'Fantastic!' he replied, adding, 'My wife is usually the one of us to make new friends.' *He's got that right*, I thought.

Lunch at the Oyster Bar at Grand Central Terminal is a scene out of another era. I half expected Don Draper to sit down right next to us and ask for a light for his Lucky Strike. Countertops loop around the perimeter, with art deco tables in the middle. We grabbed the only two seats left at the counter in front of the open kitchen. Between the view of the chefs shucking oysters and the commuters stopping at the takeout counter behind it, there would be no shortage of distraction. We each had a bowl of Manhattan clam chowder and then shared a big plate of oysters. Their aphrodisiac powers seemed to work wonders on John, as he told me in great detail of the love he had for his wife. He added that he sensed something was wrong lately, and when he said it I felt a twinge in my heart. Poor John. He seemed to realize that he had opened up a little too much and that maybe it was odd. He apologized, saying, 'There's something about spilling your woes to a stranger that feels tremendously cathartic. Want to try it? Tell me about your life.'

I shut that down right away. I couldn't tell him what I did for a living, and I couldn't bear lying to him, so I proposed a pact: we'd just talk like we were old friends, no backstory necessary. He agreed, and we settled into a lively conversation about our favorite haunts in New York, politics, and a shared love for sitting alone in the balcony of the Paris movie theater, until it was time to meet the tour.

The tour was great fun. It was filled with both little-known and fascinating tidbits that neither of us had been aware of. The guide showed us pictures of all the stars who rode the famed 20th Century back in the day. I think that was John's favorite part. Mine was the Campbell Apartment, the beautiful residence of a tycoon from the 1920s turned into a cocktail bar. It was like an interior version of a secret garden.

After the tour was over, an awkwardness that we had somehow previously avoided crept in. It was clearly time for us to go our separate ways.

'Thanks for making me come with you. I loved it. I'm going to bring my kids next time,' I said, forgetting my no-backstory rule. He jumped on it.

'Oh, so you have a family?' He smiled coyly.

I gave him a little. 'Twin girls, divorced.'

'I pity the fool who let you get away.' I smiled back. What a kind thing to say. What a nice guy. 'You know, there's a secret tennis court in this building that they didn't show us. I can get court time.' Married man asking me on a date — okay, maybe not such a nice guy. I paused, trying to figure out how to respond.

'You know, my best friend just got separated. How about in two Saturdays I bring him and my wife and we double . . . literally!'

Not a date. At least, not with him. I didn't know whether I was happy or disappointed with his honorable follow-up. *Oh my god*, I thought, *what am I doing? End this now!*

'I'm sorry, I, um, I don't date separated

men. They're never really ready to date, and I don't like being in that position.'

He responded faster than Roger Federer at the net. 'Then just you and I can play. My wife won't mind at all.'

I'm sure she wouldn't, I thought, feeling sad and awful for not being able to tell John the truth.

'Okay, let's do it,' I said. *It's just a tennis game*, I thought. *It's not like it ends in love.*

22

L'Habit ne Fait pas le Moine

By Medina Karim, Shireen's Levelheaded Sister

We arrived at Charles De Gaulle a bit later than expected. We dropped our bags at our flat and dispersed to go about our days. My father and brother went to work, my mother to shop for groceries. She instructed me and Shireen to go and collect our grandmother and bring her back home. She had been staying with our cousins on the outskirts of Paris while we were away. They live in the same neighborhood that my sister will be moving to in two weeks, after she is married. She says she might as well move back to Saudi Arabia. I know this is not true. I remind her that her fiancé is modern and even promised to teach her to drive. My sister says I am naive.

As we exit the Métro station into Paris's eighteenth arrondissement it's as if we have entered a different world. Though it's well before the start of Friday's *jumu'ah* (noon prayer), the police stand guard on closed-off streets, which will soon be filled with hundreds of faithful Muslims kneeling on their mats. There is no longer enough room inside the mosque to accommodate the worshippers. Shireen's shoulders tense at the sight of it. I don't fully understand her. If she hates being stared at as much as she always says, then I would think she would be happy to be among her own. Plus, let me explain a bit about this marriage: even though my parents arranged it, Shireen had the right to reject it. In Islam, a marriage must have consent from both the bride and the groom. The real truth is, while Shireen shares all her wild ideas and dreams with me, she would never be bold enough to go against our father. Most wouldn't. I definitely wouldn't. When my time comes, it will be easier. Shireen concerns herself with love, while I am more pragmatic about marriage. She is obsessed with never having kissed a man. Obsessed. I could care less. I never think about such things.

She turned to me and barked, 'Let's get Jeddah and go straight home.' She meant that she didn't want to linger in the area and risk running into anyone from her fiancé Fareed's family. However, it was impossible they wouldn't be there to see us, as my *jeddah* has quite a big mouth and all of Goutte d'Or probably knew that we had been on holiday in New York and that we were coming to pick her up today.

As we entered our cousin's flat I could hear from the chatter that I was right. Fareed's whole family was there. Meaning just the women, of course. After what seemed like a hundred questions about New York they turned the inquisition to Shireen and the wedding plans. As Shireen's shoulders tensed again I cut them off with the excuse of having to get home to help our mother with the laundry and tonight's meal. Shireen was very happy with me. She squeezed my hand under the table. I felt for her — I did. I had thought she would come home from this trip settled in her head about what her life would be, but she is no different from before. Maybe worse. It was close to the start of noon prayers now, and if Shireen had not wanted to run into Fareed's family, I knew she definitely did not want to run into Fareed himself on his way to the mosque. I helped my grandmother with her things and we quickly left.

When we arrived home, the house was empty and our suitcase was leaning against the door of the room we shared. I helped Jeddah, and Shireen said she would begin unpacking. After I told Jeddah nearly every detail about New York, she admitted to being tired and I suggested she nap. I looked at my watch; it had been nearly an hour since we had arrived home. I was happy to be with Jeddah, though. Last year she was never tired or out of breath. Now it seemed that she was quite often. I hated to think of the day when she would not be with us.

When I got to our bedroom door, it was locked. I banged on it, shouting through the door for Shireen to open it. She was probably annoyed that I wasn't helping her unpack and was probably eating all the chocolates we had brought back as my punishment. Finally she opened the door just a crack and peered out. Then she pulled me in quickly, slammed the door, and locked it behind me. She was dressed in what I recognized as a Chanel suit. It was ivory wool, and the skirt fell just above her knee. It had four black-and-gold buttons on the jacket with the iconic trademark C's. It was stunning. She was stunning. I had no idea what was going on. I tried to ask her, but no words came out of my mouth. She pulled out one of her fashion magazines and shoved the picture in my face. With a glee I had never seen in her, she shouted, 'Look — it's this season! This season's Chanel!' I still had no idea what was going on. She flipped open the black suitcase to reveal a treasure trove of couture. Someone else's treasure trove, for sure. She'd gone mad. I searched the outside of the suitcase, which did look a lot like ours and was shockingly shoddy compared to its couture contents, looking for a luggage tag. I opened it up. It had just a phone number on a tag that read *Pro-Travel, Beverly Hills, CA.*

'This is not ours. We have to tell someone!' I protested.

Shireen protested right back. 'No way. You will not ruin this for me,' she said. 'It's a sign.'

I was about to list every single reason that she should do what I said — and believe me, the list was long — when she pulled out of the suitcase the most perfect little black dress I had ever seen.

'Try it on!' She threw it at me.

One touch and I was gone. As I whipped off my burqa and slipped into this exquisite dress, I ran through all the things that were wrong about this scenario. Shireen turned and opened the bathroom door so the mirror faced me. I looked up self-consciously. When I saw myself, something shifted inside me. I looked beautiful. I did. It was hard to even look at myself. I tried to take control of the situation, tried to be the rational sister, as I always had been, but all that came out of my mouth were four words that I had never uttered before, words that were entirely foreign to me: 'Are there matching shoes?'

'Of course there are shoes!' she answered, digging through the suitcase to find a good pair. 'And bags too!'

She tossed me a pair of black heels and a matching bag. I slipped them on and we smiled and giggled and took turns looking in the mirror. She spoke nonsense about us sneaking out to a club on the Champs-Élysées and her getting her first kiss, but I was barely listening. I was too busy looking at the girl in the mirror. I felt giddy, I felt so glamorous and attractive. And then, as if a tidal wave had hit me, I felt horrible. I sat down on the bed and began to cry. Shireen held me.

'Don't worry,' she said. 'We won't get in trouble. It happens all the time with luggage.'

I shook my head, unable to speak what I was feeling. Barely audibly, I muttered, 'That's not it.' She looked in my eyes and she knew. She knew that I knew what she had known all along. I could tell she felt bad about it, about her part in changing my perception of our world. But really, she was not to blame. She had been filling my head with faithlessness and skepticism for as long as I can remember; it had never touched me. I knew that both Shireen and I would grow old in the tradition of our mother and grandmother. But suddenly it didn't feel like it would be enough for me. As I stood in front of the mirror in the beautiful little black dress, I knew that I was looking at a woman whom I would never see again. I wished I had never seen her in the first place, but the truth is she had always been there. I was being dishonest to myself by pretending that she hadn't.

Shireen's eyes teared up as well. 'I'm sorry,' she said quietly.

I quickly took off the shoes and the little black dress and put my burqa back on. I helped her pack up the bag. The phone rang, and somehow we knew it was the airline. We heard my mother coming up the stairs. Shireen was still wearing the Chanel suit. I quickly took her burqa off the bed and pulled it on over her head, over the suit. She laughed through watery tears. We zipped up the suitcase just as my mother came to the door to ask us about it.

'Have you unpacked your suitcase, girls? The airline is looking for a lost bag!'

'We have not,' I answered as she entered the room.

That day marked the first time I had lied to my mother, and the last time I lied to myself.

23

The Breakup

By Arthur Winters, Attorney-at-Law

It had been raining out when I'd walked into Sherri's building an hour before, and now as I left the sun was peeking through the clouds. I saw it as some kind of sign from Marilyn that I was moving in the right direction. It only helped my case that I looked particularly ridiculous today. I was wearing a slim-cut sports jacket with paisley lining and skinny jeans that Sherri had convinced me to buy a few weeks back. She said I was very close to looking hip. I said I was very close to needing a hip replacement. We laughed together for probably the last time that I can remember. We rarely got each other's jokes.

My intention when I entered her apartment was to break up with her right away, but I soon came up with a bunch of excuses to delay it. She was a girl whose father had walked out on her, and she was making up for that loss with me. It wasn't my money, although I'm sure that helped; it was my age

213

— I was simply a stand-in father figure. This had a lot to do with the reason I hadn't broken up with her sooner. I didn't want to be another older man who left her. Plus I'd always hoped she would tire of me before this conversation would have to take place. I looked into her eyes and tried to gather my nerve.

Her eyes were so young-looking; they were often the thing that embarrassed me most about our age difference. Not her girlish figure, her luminous smile, or her soft skin, which had seen nearly half the sunny days that mine had, with twice the sunblock. It was her eyes. She had yet to develop the tiny lines that eventually spring out from the corners of people's eyes like sunbeams signaling age, but also life. Whoever named those lines crow's feet did them a huge etymological disservice. If they called them eagle's feet, maybe they'd be worn like a badge of honor. I've come to see that recently. I never thought about it with Marilyn — we grew older together. But I see more beauty in eyes that have seen things. When I looked into Sherri's youthful eyes, I saw an old man with a girl half his age. I saw the truth. I liked Felicia's eyes. I realized that was the gist of what I had to explain to her.

She beat me to the punch. 'Is something going on?' she asked, adding that she'd noticed that I had been distant lately. She'd have to be dense not to have noticed. I jumped on it, explaining to her, kindly, that I was worried I was wasting her time and that while I want to marry again, I want it to be to an equal, a teammate, not a trophy wife. Someone who's at my stage in life, who's had some of the same experiences, maybe. And then her young eyes started to cry and I felt bad. But she cried just a little bit, and really, just like that it was over. It was nothing compared to the histrionics that had surrounded that little black dress.

I handed her my handkerchief and she wiped her eyes with it. Afterward she straightened it out and ran her fingers over my initials sewn into the corner.

'Can I keep it?' she asked.

'Of course,' I responded.

I was surprised and touched by her sentiment, but as I left her building, the only real emotion I felt was relief.

24

I Love New York!

By Sally Ann Fennely,
Runway Model / New New Yorker

New York City had quickly grown on me, and as the rules of southern hospitality demanded, I returned the favor and grew on it right back. It wasn't at all subtle, like the way you fall in love with the South, real slow on a hot August day, sipping sweet tea from a Mason jar. It was quick. Two shots of Patrón with a Red Bull chaser at the rooftop bar of the Standard Hotel and I was gone. And believe you me, this wasn't just some one-night stand. It was reaffirmed at the corner bagel shop the next morning. True love schmeared between two halves of my first warm-from-the-oven everything bagel. So long, grits!

From then on I fell in love on a near-daily basis. And lucky me, the feeling was mutual! I think New York City first started falling in love with me on account of my accent; the very accent that I had spent my first weeks swallowing with my morning coffee was just the thing that ended up making people fuss over me. Turns out that people weren't as judgmental as I first thought. By and by, most folks that I came across found me entertaining. *Delightful* was actually the word they used most. 'Your accent is *delightful*.' Sometimes it was *refreshing*, often *charming*, and once even *enchanting*.

And just like that, New York was crushing on Sally Ann Fennely. Not on account of my long legs and perfect smile and wavy blond hair, though I'm sure all that opened doors. But it was what I said and how I said it that got me invited in. It meant so much to me to know that it wasn't just on account of my looks. As soon as I realized it, I began to lay it on heavier than a cow in a cotton field. Sounds pretty charming, right? A cow in a cotton field? Well, guess what, that's not even a thing. I just made it up right on the spot. That cow in that cotton field was just the kind of thing that had people going on about how refreshing and real I was.

I first noticed the reaction at dinner in the women's boardinghouse where I live. Yes, there are still women's boardinghouses in New York City. When word first came in that I'd been accepted at the modeling agency, my mama, who had been pushing me all along, began to backpedal. Suddenly spooked at the reality of me living in the big city, she started Googling statistics on crime rates and the air-quality index — this from a woman who spent half her life with a cigarette dangling from her lips. But my grandma had a plan. She was a big Sylvia Plath fan and told us all about how when Sylvia Plath moved to New York she lived in a women's boardinghouse, a safe place called the Barbizon. She even wrote about it in *The Bell Jar*. Somehow this risky analogy worked, as if suicidal Sylvia Plath had the makings of a role model.

The Barbizon was long closed, but there were about ten others to choose from; I ended up renting a room at a boardinghouse on the Upper West Side that supplied two meals a day and had a house mother and a twenty-four-hour doorman. Plus there was a strict no-boys policy. Mama was thrilled, and to be honest, I was happy about it too. I didn't feel any more grown up or capable of living alone than I had the day before finding out I would be a runway model. The whole setup sounded more like a college sorority than life in the big city — though when I got here, no one seemed very sisterly to me. Well, at least not straightaway.

The first week at dinner I sat with the wrong girls — two other models, who barely introduced themselves and spent the entire meal discussing whether you can really wear black and navy together. (You can.) As the next week began I was late for dinner on account of my neighbor being busted for sneaking a boy up to her room. The matron was in the hallway pitching a conniption fit, and I was too frightened to try and slip by. When I finally made it down, I sat at the only seat available, between two smart-looking girls.

I must have looked a fright, 'cause they came right out and asked me what was the matter. Forgetting my efforts to subdue my southern accent, I blurted out, 'That matron is madder than a wet hen!' They started to laugh. At first I thought they were making fun of me. My blushing cheeks must have given it away, 'cause the dark-haired girl, Margot, jumped right in and turned it around.

'What a great expression, 'madder than a wet hen.' I have to write that down!'

Turns out that she and the other girl, Halle, worked at *New York* magazine as interns. They didn't get paid much, but they were invited to everything. One was from no farther away than Brooklyn, but her parents had wanted her to move out, and the other was from Boston.

I don't know if they were honing their

journalistic skills or if they were just nosy, but they sure did ask a lot of questions. 'Where are you from?' 'Why is a wet hen so mad?' 'What are southern boys like?' 'What do you do for kicks in Alabama?' I tried to sound interesting, but it was real hard. I didn't imagine that tales of cotton farming and Friday night football would interest them. Luckily they *loved* my accent. It seemed that listening to me talk and hearing about a place they'd never been interested them plenty. That was the first time that I thought maybe I would stay in this big noisy city with a zillion people in it. Friends can really make any place seem livable, I think. The trick is to find a few of your own, and by the end of that dinner I felt like I had.

One night Margot got three seats to a Broadway musical through work and took Halle and me along. The first thing my grandma had said when we got word about me coming to New York was that I should go see a big musical on Broadway. She said it was something she had always wanted to do but she had never had the chance. I felt so grateful and excited to be going and a little bad that my grandma never had. I vowed to remember every last detail and relay them all to her on our Sunday call. My excitement was slightly squashed once we got to our seats.

Turns out my friends' editor's son and a friend of his were in the seats next to us, and they were kind of cocky. Before the show even started they asked us to join them for dinner after at a famous old theater-district restaurant called Sardi's. Thanks to Wikipedia and the crazy long line for the ladies' room at intermission, I found out that Sardi's is famous for having hundreds of stars' caricatures on its walls. That sounded fine and all, but I really didn't care for these two boys. The more they spoke, the stupider they seemed, like they didn't even have the sense they were born with. Margot insisted we had to go on account of wanting to make a good impression on her boss, and Halle said we should go 'cause it would be fun. So we did. But it wasn't.

Halfway between the appetizers and the main course, and well on my way to the realization that I was the fifth wheel, I excused myself to 'go tee-tee,' a line that usually had Margot and Halle in stitches, but this time they were so busy trying to impress these nincompoops that I got nothing. As I passed the bar, I decided to prolong my absence by sitting down and ordering a cosmopolitan. I didn't even know what was in one, just that it was pink. Like most girls my age, the sum total of my knowledge of what to do in a Manhattan bar came from watching reruns of *Sex and the City*. The older man sitting next to me was dressed like he was someone important, but he was a bit liquored up. He was drawing a pitchfork and devil horns on a photo in *New York*.

'My girlfriends work for *New York*,' I said, channeling my inner Carrie Bradshaw.

'I have nothing against the magazine,' he said, slurring a little, 'just this nightmare of a woman!' He shoved the picture toward me.

Under his devil scrawls was, according to the caption, an actress from *That Southern Play*. But it was the strangest of coincidences. I looked closer. There was no question: the actress was wearing *my* dress! Well, not my dress, really, but the one that got my picture on the front of *Women's Wear Daily* and a host of modeling jobs to boot.

'That's my dress!' I exclaimed proudly.

He plopped down his glass for a refill, and the bartender reluctantly poured him another while explaining to me, 'Don't mind him — he produced what was to be the hottest play of the season and his actress flew the coop.'

'That's awful,' I said, 'cause it was.

'*She* was awful,' he answered. 'She did a horrible southern accent, and her reviews were dreadful. I hired her only because the investors pushed me to. I'll never do that again.'

'Like my grandma always says, you lie down with dogs, you wake up with fleas.' I looked at the desecrated picture again and added, in full southern drawl, 'Bless her heart.'

Hearing my accent, he didn't seem to know if I was for real or was just mocking him, so he asked me, 'What are you doing at this bar? Did someone send you over here to audition?'

'Audition? Why, no, sir. I'm just getting away from two boys who think the sun comes up just to hear 'em crow.'

The producer's eyes popped out. 'Who sent you? Stephen Schwartz? Nathan Lane? That is quite a heavy accent you got there!'

'Heavier than a cow in a cotton field!' I told him.

And so it was that right there at Sardi's I auditioned for my first part on the Broadway stage for the producer of *That Southern Play*. Soon I'll make my Broadway debut! Not too shabby for an Alabama girl.

I don't mean to sound like a T-shirt, but really, I love New York!

25

In Too Deep
at the Ostrich Detective Agency

By Andie Rand, Private Detective

The tennis match at Grand Central was great in that we were perfectly matched. I wondered if John and Caroline played together. I thought of them playing on summer weekends wherever it is that they summer and a weird pang of jealousy followed. It took a lot of self-control not to ask him about it. Bringing her up as if I didn't know her would make my deception feel even more appalling. I resisted the urge. He had to run afterward but asked to see me again.

'I'm showing *North by Northwest* in class this week. You should come.'

I responded with a quizzical look; I didn't know what *North by Northwest* had to do with anything.

'They spoke about it on our Grand Central tour, remember? Alfred Hitchcock, Cary Grant, Eva Marie Saint?' I didn't, but his enthusiasm was catching and also quite adorable.

I smiled. 'Enough said.'

* * *

That's how I found myself a couple of days later in a classroom for the first time in twenty years. It was fun — it made me feel like a college student again, when everything was ahead of me, no broken marriage behind me. John gave a brief introduction, then darkened the room, and as the opening credits started, he made his way up to where I was sitting and sat down right next to me. 'Glad you could make it,' he whispered before settling down in his seat. I was a bit worried that I wouldn't be able to concentrate, sitting in the dark like this with John, but the movie sucked me right in. After it was over he mixed a few questions about Grand Central into his lecture — things we had learned on our tour. Each time, his eyes found mine, coaxing me to answer. And when I did, I felt such a strong connection to him, two people in a sea of strangers with a secret.

'Which other Hitchcock film used both Grand Central and Penn Station?'

'*Spellbound!*' I answered, barely waiting for him to call on me.

I was so eager that a couple of students in the row ahead turned around to look at me, as though wondering what I was doing there. And when I saw their faces, I realized that I didn't know what I was doing there myself. I shouldn't have come. I was falling for a married man to whom I was being completely dishonest, and who'd repeatedly talked about his commitment to his (lying, cheating) wife. I decided I would not stick around for coffee after class, as I had promised, and vowed never to see him again.

But two Sundays later I broke my vow. It was my weekend off, and damn if I wasn't again sitting in my office following John Westmont's whereabouts on my computer. Okay, if I'm totally honest, I'd checked in on him nearly every day since I had sworn I wouldn't, but on the tracking device — I didn't and wouldn't go so far as to retrieve his e-mails from my junk folder. Obeying that one rule left me feeling less out of control. Still, he had become an obsession. More like an addiction. John Westmont was my heroin. Our few encounters had left me hooked and wanting more.

That day he was walking the High Line. I know, you're probably thinking this guy is really into landmarks, but I can tell you this is the only remotely touristy thing he had done over those past two weeks. Most nights he was home at his Fifth Avenue apartment, which by the way is so palatial it covers two locations on the tracking device. It's hard to imagine such a down-to-earth guy coming from such affluence. Most of his days were spent in or around Columbia University. Last Sunday he went to Madison Square Garden, for the Knicks game, I assume. Thursday he attended a conference at the Paley Center for Media, and this past Wednesday he saw the afternoon movie at the Paris Theatre. It took every bit of self-control I could summon not to show up in that balcony and casually sit next to him. I daydreamed about what I would say. *Will you quit following me!* Or *Not you again!* How he would offer me some of his popcorn and how my hand would brush against his when we inevitably reached into the bucket at the same time. Within minutes of reimagining the missed popcorn scenario I found myself on the street hailing a cab, like the junkie I am.

A few years back the city reinvented the High Line, taking the abandoned elevated freight rail line and landscaping it, turning it into a long narrow stretch of park along the West Side of Manhattan. It's a pretty great addition. The little green dot on my computer indicated that John had started at the 34th

Street entrance and was heading downtown; therefore I would start in the meatpacking district at the Gansevoort Street entrance and head up. Eventually, if we both continued on our course, we would bump right into each other. If not, it was beautiful out, and a good walk and fresh air never hurt anyone. Or so I thought.

About ten blocks in, I caught a glimpse of him. It made my heart gasp a bit. I wished I didn't feel this way about this man I barely knew whom it could be a career-derailing disaster to have a relationship with. He was a good-looking guy in an everyday way. He looked like Gary Cooper or Greg Kinnear. He was sweet, very sweet and old-fashioned, which I loved. He was smart and very thoughtful. All those things are great — but as I watched him order ice cream from a vendor, I began to wonder whether I really liked him or just wanted to stick it to his cheating wife, thus indirectly sticking it to my cheating husband. The vendor handed him a cone. Could that be what this is all about: some kind of vindictive, psychological infidelity transference? Am I just feeling for him because he is about to experience the same pain that I did? I should have seen a shrink when everyone suggested it three years ago. 'Don't hang on to this anger,' they said. 'Talk to someone.'

The ice cream vendor handed John a second cone. Two cones. Two cones. It took a minute for it to sink in. Then up walked a smiling Caroline Westmont. I don't know why I never considered this possibility — I guess because she was cheating on him, or had been at least, and he always seemed to be alone. I looked for an extra few seconds at what appeared to be a happy couple. Maybe she had changed her mind, straightened out her ways. One glance in my direction by either of them and I was done. I turned and ran the other way.

I went back to my office and deleted John Westmont's little green dot from my tracking portal. That was it: all connections severed. I was determined to stay clean.

26

Flip Flop

By Natalie, the Beard

It was a slow morning in the store, which is unusual this close to Christmas. The only action at all was that my little black Max Hammer dress came back from being loaned out to Jordana Winston. I still call it mine, though at this point its line of succession is quite far-reaching; it arrived neatly folded in a box from Paris, of all places, although it looked more like it had hitched a ride home with a French sailor. I personally steamed it out in the back, but, sadly, I decided it was a goner. It was stretched out, stained, and had generally just seen too much action. The Max Hammer people would take it back because it had been loaned out for publicity.

As I wrote out the return slip I felt a twinge of nostalgia for the dress and everything that had happened. Why was I so stubborn about Jeremy? Why couldn't I accept his apology? Maybe I was hiding behind the whole misunderstanding because I was scared of getting hurt again. Under 'reason for return' I wrote, *Damaged*. I should hang the same tag on myself, I thought. I hung the dress in the back and attached the slip for Ruthie to authorize when she came in later. That was some dress. I loved how I felt in it.

Getting dressed up like that, in a really special dress, brings back memories of playing dress-up as a kid. My sister and I had a box filled with princess costumes and old communion dresses that my mom picked up here and there to add to our collection. We would prance around in them with fake pearls, white gloves, and my mom's old heels. I think that little-girl pastime, dressing up and pretending to be a bride or a princess, or just a grownup, really sets the stage for how a beautiful dress makes a woman feel as an adult. Maybe it's just that I'm still young, but whenever I dress, really dress, a part of me feels like it's all make-believe — like anything could happen.

A slow day at work really allows one's mind to drift, and mine was drifting all over the place. Luckily I had Tomás to engage me. Ruthie is fun to be on with when it's crowded — she's queen of the side-eye and one-liner, and her running commentary can be hilarious. But when it's quiet, Tomás is my guy. When you're on with Ruthie on a slow day, she gives you a lot of breaks, which for her hold the promise of another cigarette. She'll say, 'Go take an extra break,' so she can take extra breaks, which end up costing me extra money as I wander around the store making mental notes of everything I want to buy with my next paycheck. With Tomás we both generally just stick it out on the floor together. To make the time go faster we'll play games like guess who or I spy. On that day we played I spy, because we were both exhausted and didn't have the brainpower for anything more. It was his turn.

'I spy with my tired bloodshot eye something blue.' He looked at me with a sad face, and I got that he was talking about my mood. He was quite observant, Tomás. We'd become really close friends lately.

'I'm fine. Please play for real. I don't want to think about anything today.'

'Fine. I spy with my tired bloodshot eye something else blue.' He looked in the direction of a passing customer and I laughed.

'I see it,' I said. It was the head of one of those naturally gray-haired women who dye their own hair and don't seem to notice that it's blue — a little late in life for a punk-rock stage.

My turn. I looked out the window. 'I spy

with my little eye something . . . cracked.'

'Is it that little crack on Lexington that you used when we played last week?'

'Actually it is, but take a look — it's huge. It nearly crosses the whole street!'

He looked. 'Wow, someone should say something about that to someone.'

'Someone should. You're up.'

He turned his attention back to the interior of the store. '*Dios mio!*' he cried. 'I spy your short, shallow, and now shameless ex-boyfriend.'

I followed his line of sight. 'I goddamn see it. Ugh. Game over.'

Flip Roberts walked directly toward us through the dress department. He had come in with the excuse of buying his wife a gift. It was the first time that I had seen him since Turks and Caicos and, more important, the first time the sight of him hadn't rocked me to my core.

I called him right out on his reason for being there. 'Really, Flip? There are like a thousand places to buy a gift in this city — '

He interrupted me with what he thought was a joke: 'Out of all the dress joints in all the towns in all the world, he walks into mine.' It was just the kind of clever thing that I would have laughed at when I was dating him. Now it just seemed hopelessly unoriginal . . . like him.

'I really came to see you,' he said disingenuously. 'I assume from the photo on Page Six this morning that you and your boyfriend broke up, and I just wanted to see if you were doing okay.'

What photo on Page Six? I couldn't hide my shock, or the fact that the thought of a photo of Jeremy with another woman made me want to throw up, so I spun it.

'You're a married man, Flip! Do you really think your wife would appreciate your checking in on your old girlfriend like this?'

'She doesn't know I'm here.' His response was pathetic.

'I figured as much,' I said disapprovingly.

'I haven't stopped thinking about you since we bumped into each other, and when I saw the *Post* this morning, well, I thought maybe — '

I really didn't care what he thought, and I wanted to make that clear. I interrupted him. 'I'm glad you came in,' I said, rather cruelly. His face lit up. 'I've been wanting to thank you.'

'Thank me?' he asked, confused but hopeful. I couldn't believe I'd ever had it so bad for this guy — he was such a tool.

'Yes. If you hadn't realized that something was lacking in our relationship, I might have spent my whole life with you — my whole life feeling less than, when really I am so much more than. Thanks to you, I didn't settle for that.'

He jumped at the bait. 'But you're not less than, you're incredible, and I was just too stuck on some snobby version of who I thought I deserved to marry.'

'Who you deserve to marry? I can tell you one thing, you don't deserve me! Go home to your wife, Flip.' I walked away with tears in my eyes and made a beeline for the dressing room. But I wasn't crying over Flip Roberts. I was crying over Jeremy.

After our parting in Turks and Caicos he had called nearly every day. At first his messages were about wanting to win the fight, wanting to be right. Then they turned apologetic. And the last one just said, 'I will always miss you but won't bother you anymore.' It had been a week since then. While I was drawing this out like some kind of Greek tragedy, he was playing the Hollywood version and moving on.

Tomás knocked on the dressing-room door. He was carrying the paper. 'Sorry,' he said. 'Do you want to see it for yourself?' There in black and white was Jeremy lip-locked to a woman on a ski lift in Vermont. The caption read, 'Snowbound!'

I let out a spontaneous roar, unable to stop myself from laughing at the joke. 'This is from his new movie, *Snowbound*!' I said, still smiling, tears of happiness filling my eyes. 'That's his costar, not his girlfriend!'

Tomás had tears in his eyes too. He's such a good friend. And such a romantic! 'Are you sure?' he whimpered.

'Of course I am — I read this script. I ran the lines in this scene with him.'

'You should go, Natalie — go get him!'

His energy was catching. I thought about it, running right up to Vermont and into Jeremy's arms. But that stuff didn't happen in real life. And I don't even drive.

'I have no idea where this was taken, and I can't just barge onto the set. I'll wait for him to get back.'

But Tomás wasn't having it. He looked at the picture again. 'What if he falls for her? Look at her. Even I might fall for her.'

I looked at the picture. He did have a point. 'Even *I* might fall for her!' We laughed as I considered my options.

'I have his publicist's card in my wallet from that photo shoot.' I pulled it out. His office was right around the corner.

Tomás grabbed it from me. 'Let's go in person!'

'But the floor isn't covered!'

'Love trumps a lady needing a different size.' He grabbed my hand.

'You should stay. We could get fired!' I protested.

'No way!' he protested louder. 'I'm your ride-or-die chick!'

I laughed the whole way there.

27

For She's a Jolly Good Fellow

By Arthur Winters, Attorney-at-Law

It turns out that it took all of two interviews for Felicia to get another job, and so it was that in the blink of an eye I was sitting at my desk trying to compose a toast in her honor. Everything was set for the party. I did it all myself and I really went all out, though I had to be careful. There are company rules and budgets for such things, and I didn't want anyone to catch on to our relationship. I filled the room with celebration cakes from Payard and bottles of Veuve Clicquot and bought her a beautiful bouquet of flowers from her favorite florist. Writing the toast turned out to be the most difficult task. I didn't know what to say. *Good luck, thank you, goodbye*. Every word I chose but the last seemed trite. It bothered me that after all this time together at work my words would seem generic. Not to the room, but to Felicia. Time was up, and I shoved my note card in my breast pocket and headed to the party.

Even with the standard two weeks' notice, I was completely unprepared for Felicia's departure. Deep down I was happy for her and glad that our relationship would soon be out in the open, but my misery at the thought of not seeing her all day masked it. It seems her competence and loyalty had landed her a job at one of the most prestigious law firms in the city. The office was down on Wall Street, far away from midtown, and every time I thought of the distance between the two, a lump formed in my throat. I really had to pull myself together.

I entered the room and downed my first glass of champagne to calm my nerves. Everyone was chatting and milling about, and the time went quickly. Before long the type-A people that made up our firm wanted to get back to work. They encouraged me to make my toast.

I began with the words on my note card.

'I want to say a few words on behalf of everyone at Canner, Silfen, Sheanshang, and Winters, to express our appreciation for Felicia's unmatched term of dedicated service. Felicia has spent eighteen years with us, and in that time she has served as an example of excellence to everyone around her, foremost myself.'

So far I was keeping my composure. But as I paused to allow the new associates their obligatory laugh, it gave me time to catch Felicia's eye, and I started to lose it. I fumbled with my card and begged myself to get it together as I continued with the words I had written.

'Felicia, for eighteen years I have walked off the elevator and been greeted by your smile.' My voice cracked and I felt moisture building up in my eyes. 'I . . . I can't imagine not seeing . . . that smile every day . . . ' I squeezed my eyes tight, but it was too late; a tear had escaped. One sizable lone tear. The sight of it set off murmurs across the room, and nearly every woman took my cue and welled up too. At this point they were probably sad to see Felicia go and happy that a boss could cry over his assistant's departure. I found Felicia's eyes again and it was over. The tears were pouring down her face. I couldn't bear it, any of it. I was sixty years old. I had lost the first love of my life already; I wasn't about to waste any more time. I tossed my note card over my shoulder and got down on one knee.

'Felicia, I refuse to spend even one more day apart from you. If you are no longer going to work for me, would you please do me the honor of becoming my wife?'

Her reply nearly bowled me over as everyone shouted and cheered.

'Yes. Yes!' she cried.

Suddenly I became very conscious of the fact that I had just cried and proposed in front of a roomful of my colleagues. I followed with a sheepish joke: 'I guess the cat's out of the bag.'

Everyone laughed and toasted our long, happy life together. My partners had the company limo brought around and we were escorted out, along with the extra bottles of champagne, by nearly everyone in the firm.

We sank into our seats and caught our breath.

'Where to, Mr. Winters?'

I had no idea. 'Let me ask my fiancée.' It felt so good to say it out loud — my fiancée, soon to be my wife.

Felicia seemed to enjoy it as well. She laughed and said, 'We never did walk across the Brooklyn Bridge!'

28

Tell Hank They Beat It Out of Me

By Albert, Jeremy's Publicist

They came busting into my office like Bonnie and Clyde on crack. My intern followed them, trying to stop them, but she didn't stand a chance.

'Don't worry, Devan, it's okay. Hello, Natalie, nice to see you again.' I was pleasant, partially because I had liked her when we met and mostly because of the tall drink of water that was her escort. I was single again, and this Latin guy was gorgeous. (Natalie and Jeremy weren't the only couple who didn't survive the Tab Hunter scandal, as we had taken to calling it.) 'What can I do for you?' I asked, though I had a feeling this involved today's *New York Post*.

Natalie was nervous, so the tall drink of water spoke for her, introducing himself first. 'Hi, I'm Tomás. Natalie wants to surprise Jeremy on set but doesn't know where that is, so we were hoping that you could tell us.' He was pretty gorgeous and definitely gay, but there was no way I was pulling back on this thing; I had leaked that photo to Page Six myself and was sticking with the illusion of Jeremy and his new girl. The caption said nothing but the name of the movie. People could assume anything they wanted.

'I'm sorry to tell you, though I think it's pretty obvious from the picture, Jeremy has moved on. Just a happy couple kissing on the slopes.'

Tomás looked as if he would cry, but Natalie from Astoria wasn't buying it. 'I don't believe you,' she said. 'There's no way he got over me so quickly, and I read the script for *Snowbound*. I remember the scene.'

She was right, of course. I'd sworn I was done staging things after the red-carpet fiasco, but when the movie's publicist sent me the photo yesterday, I hit Forward and sent it over to my guy at the *Post*, partly to make it up to him for the red-carpet pix that never materialized and partly to solidify my boy's sexual orientation among the doubters. A picture is always worth a thousand words, even if it is just a publicity still.

I hated myself for it, but I denied her denial. She had had her chance with him, and I would happily have gone with their story if it had worked out on its own — the truth is always easier than the made-up stuff. But this girl had played with Jeremy's head — I had seen it firsthand — and he needed to concentrate on his career. It was best for me to scare her off, I was sure of it. I kissed goodbye any chance of hooking up with Tomás and stuck to my guns.

'It's true that they're filming a movie together, but the romance is real. He's a big Hollywood star. What did you expect?'

Her eyes filled with tears. 'But he's not like that!' she cried. 'He always made *me* feel like the star.'

Oh, for the love of Bette Midler, why'd she have to go and say that? She understood what was so special about him: it wasn't his looks or his smile or his swagger, it was the way he brought out the good in everyone around him. He did it onscreen and he did it in person. She got him, and it broke me.

'He's staying at the Inns at the Equinox in Manchester, Vermont. She's not his girl-friend. He didn't get over you — he can't even say your name.' I buzzed Devan. 'Devan, have the company car meet us on Third Avenue. And tell the driver to fill up the tank. We're all going to Vermont.'

Tomás's face lit up. 'All?'

I smiled. 'The more, the merrier!' adding to save face, 'It's a closed set — you'll never get in without me.'

Natalie hugged me and kissed me all over my face. Tomás was tickled pink. She looked at him, then back at me, and winked.

'Maybe it'll be happy endings all around!'

29

#DrinkTheKoolAid

By Sophie Stiner, Brown Graduate

I was all set to attend the Christie's holiday party that night when a text from Thea Baxter derailed me.

Be a doll and let me borrow that Max Hammer you wore to the library benefit?

I couldn't believe she was so last-minute. I'd had my outfit set since the day she invited me. I had been careful to pick something classic and modest. I didn't want my clothes to define me in any way. Damn. I doubted that dress was still at Bloomingdale's.

I could have texted her right back saying that it was at the cleaner's, but I knew that lending her the dress would balance the favor scale between us. I know that logically a dress can't compare to a possible job, but this really was some dress. She would turn heads in it. And I needed to do whatever it took to get a job. So I decided I would run to Bloomingdale's in hopes of finding it, buy it on my mom's emergency credit card, and return it within the billing cycle. I would need to delay responding to her text in case my plan didn't work. I needed an aligram.

Aligram is a word I made up: part alibi, part Instagram, an aligram is when you use social media to back up a lie. Posting a photo that serves to confirm an excuse, or your supposed whereabouts. I threw my fluffy white terry robe over my clothes, pulled my hair off my face with a thick headband, and snapped a picture.

#IHeartMassages #Bliss @Bliss

I now had the time a ninety-minute massage would take to either find the dress or send back an apologetic *Sorry I didn't text back sooner, at bliss spa.* ☹ *dress at cleaners.*

I ran to Bloomingdale's, practically breaking my neck on a huge crack in the pavement while crossing Lexington Avenue. When I got there, the dress department was empty. There was actually no one there to help me. Everything seemed to be going against me today, and I was running out of time. I should've included a mani-pedi in my aligram. I searched all over and was about to give up when an older woman who smelled a bit like my Grandma Freda, a pleasant mix of Shalimar and Marlboro Lights with a slight hint of fried onions, approached me. She was quite apologetic and very surprised that the department was empty. She seemed like one of those hardcore women who had worked there forever, a lifer who took real pride in her job. I had a feeling that if anyone could help me, it would be her.

'Where the hell is everybody?' she said under her breath; then, more professionally, 'I'm so sorry, can I help you with something?'

'More like everything!' I said, immediately throwing myself on her mercy. She seemed like the straightforward type, so I came right out and explained my predicament. Including that it was nearly Christmas, that I had yet to find a job, and that the Max Hammer dress might be just the break I needed. She was honest in return.

'I have one size small in the back, but it's a mess, and it's set to go back to the manufacturer.'

'Can I buy it today and return it tomorrow?' I asked, playing up my sheepishness, hoping she would take pity on me.

She took a beat and agreed. 'Sure, to make up for no one being here to help you.' She put a finger to her lips. 'But mum's the word. There are major rules about that lately.'

'Mum's the word,' I repeated as she went off to get it.

Maybe my luck was changing. I hoped so. Tonight was beginning to feel like my last chance. I am nearly twenty-three, you know.

As she rung me up I responded to Thea Baxter:

Of course, sorry for the delay. Should I leave it with my doorman?

She answered as if she'd been waiting by the phone, though she struck me as the type who always was.

Yay!!!!! Yes, text me your address.

40 East 71st. I need it back for a wedding this weekend.

I'll drop it back in the a.m. Who's getting married?

My boyfriend's BFF from Choate. I think he's a Kennedy.

What the hell is wrong with me?

Wow! GTG. See you tonight.

I had so convinced myself that I actually worked for Sotheby's that I felt a twinge of guilt upon entering the Christie's soirée. I mean, work there or not, everyone in the art world knows that Sotheby's and Christie's are in daily competition. Every prominent piece of art heading for auction, as well as every collector, is fair game for one or the other. The art market, flat or exciting, high or low, is determined by what goes on at these two houses. Last year it was Sotheby's that ended up on top in annual sales, mostly because of its acquisition of one mammoth Impressionist estate. For the few years prior Christie's had been ahead. From the looks of this party, it seemed Christie's was going to great lengths to get back on top. Including trying to steal away some cool new blood with excellent taste and, might I add, a following on Instagram that as of party time had reached, wait for it . . . 1700 followers. Finally things were coming together. Soon I would be buying a little black dress for keeps to hang in my very own closet in my very own crib. *Crib* — I felt awkward even thinking the word. I was so not cool.

Thea Baxter came running over with open arms. She gave me a quick hug and spun around. 'I love this dress. I wish I could keep it!'

I laughed a compulsory laugh. 'Remember, I'm wearing it to that wedding this weekend — you promised.'

'I promise,' she said with a pout.

I felt a strange allegiance to the saleslady at Bloomingdale's. I wasn't sure if it was because she smelled like my Grandma Freda or because she seemed so dedicated to her job, but I didn't want to break my word. Whatever it is that my word meant at this point.

'So how are things over at Sotheby's?' Thea said *Sotheby's* in a weird voice usually reserved for impressions of Satan.

'Same old.' I brushed off her question as if she couldn't possibly be looking for a real answer. But it worked — she moved on.

'Let's get some bubbly and then I'll introduce you to my boss, Sheldra Fine.' She led me to the bar as she talked about the things you talk about when you see someone with whom your only connection is your alma mater. Benign questions, like *Did you hear that so-and-so got engaged?* or *that so-and-so is in rehab?* She was so basic.

Just as we were running out of nothingness she caught the eye of her boss and we were summoned over. The boss was the kind of woman that my grandmother would describe as handsome. She spoke in a monotone: 'Hello, Sophie. Thea has told me so much about you.' I smiled, thinking, *Thea doesn't know so much about me.*

She took a step back and looked me over from head to toe, purposefully, not discreetly. She asked, 'Whom do you consider more innovative, Shiraga or Yves Klein?'

Please, so easy. 'Shiraga painted with his feet years earlier than Klein used his body.'

She didn't react. 'Shinzo or Kikuji?' she asked.

'Eiko,' I responded with a confident smile.

'A photographer? And don't say Moriyama or Kawauchi.'

I smirked, as I had what I knew was a great answer. 'Fan Ho. For his drama and simplicity.'

'Hmmm. I like your style. Call me Monday morning to set up a formal interview.'

Thea was more excited than I was. 'You nailed it. Let's do a shot!' she shrieked as soon as her boss was out of earshot. We both sat down. 'Two shots of Patrón, please,' she asked the bartender before I'd even agreed. As we toasted I held up my phone and took a selfie. We checked it before we drank, in case we needed a redo.

'You can't post that!' she quickly objected.

'Why? You look great!'

'It says Christie's behind us!' she said, alarmed.

'So?'

'So it will raise suspicion!'

'I'm quitting anyway. What's the difference?'

She looked at me like I was a total moron. 'Obviously Sheldra is going to want you to do some spying before you leave — you know, some internal espionage,' she said, without humor.

'Who are you, Edwina Snowden?' I said, laughing at my own joke. 'I can't spy for you!' Of course I meant I actually couldn't spy, because I had no way of getting into the building, but I wouldn't have spied on Sotheby's even if I could have.

I had begun to Instagram the pic when she grabbed my phone away from me. 'I'm serious, Sophie!'

I got serious too. Somehow the fact that I'd been lying made me even more self-righteous.

'Listen, Thea, it's one thing for me to leave Sotheby's but quite another to screw them over in the process. If Sheldra doesn't want me for my style and my knowledge, then I'm out.'

'Then I guess you're out,' Thea said as she placed her still-full shot glass back on the bar and stormed off. I laughed at my ambiguous principles. I guess it was one thing to quit a fake job but quite another to be the kind of girl who would fake-screw my employer. In a strange way it felt good to hold on to my values, convoluted as they may be.

The man beside me hijacked Thea's shot and raised it to toast. 'To you!'

I clicked his glass and we drank. 'Why are we drinking to me?' I asked upon recovering from the burn.

'I don't often see that kind of integrity in young people. I'm impressed.'

I thanked him as he ordered us another round.

'Was she a good friend?' he asked curiously.

'Not really,' I said, playing with the rim of my glass. 'She wasn't really my type — a snob, and for no reason. She was a slush-fund baby.'

'You mean a trust-fund baby?'

'No, a slush-fund baby — her father paid for her entire education by stealing from his company's petty cash.'

He laughed spontaneously from his gut. *Hmmm, I'm cool* and *funny*.

'I wish I was in the art game. I would snatch you right up.'

'What do you do?' I asked, more out of courtesy than because I cared.

'I own a marketing company, DrinkTheK-oolAid.com,' he said, as if I should have heard of it. My face must have given me away.

254

'Drink is made up of a group of influencers. We bring ideas to the mainstream consciousness through social media. It's like reality television for the three-second attention span.'

I laughed. 'That's actually what I do!'

He asked me to explain, so I went on to describe the road that led me to the seat at the bar next to him. Everything from my very first aligram to borrowing the little black dress from Bloomingdale's in a last-ditch effort to keep up appearances. As I told the story I realized how much I had enjoyed the whole trip. Not the lying, but the creativity involved in getting the right photo, choosing the right caption, and the instant and constant gratification of the likes and new followers. I was good at it. It was actually what kept me from sinking into a depression through all the rejections of my unsuccessful job search. He ate it all up and promised me that if I came to work for him, I could hashtag my way to a crib of my own in no time.

'You put on a good show,' he said. 'Right down to your red-bottomed shoes.'

I kept that one lie to myself: my red soles were courtesy of a very resourceful shoe-maker on 82nd and Third and not, as my #IHeartLouboutin preparty post would lead my followers to believe, the genuine article.

As far as the finest little black dresses were concerned, he promised me that designers would be dropping them at my doorstep in the hope of the right tweet or the right photo. He wanted me to help him co-opt an entire generation — my generation — of doe-eyed followers. Who was I to say no? In the past that was an honor bestowed on cultural icons like Andy Warhol and Oprah, but now it seems that I, Sophie Stiner, am cool enough to lead the way.

Go ahead and tag me! @SophieStiner @DrinkThe KoolAid #dreamjob #cool

30

Snowbound Bound

By Natalie, the Beard

I was so nervous that when we settled into the limo I began biting my nails, and I wasn't even a nail-biter. I wanted to chicken out, call the whole thing off, but one look at Albert and Tomás and I realized that this road trip was no longer entirely about me. In fact, from the way they were looking at each other I calculated my relevance to be at about 10 percent. This was confirmed by Tomás's enthusiastic announcement of our first scheduled stop: a quick lunch at Miss Florence Diner, just outside Northampton, Massachusetts. Before I could say anything, or even ask if it was on the way, Albert blurted out with equal enthusiasm, 'Oh my god, I've never been to Northampton!'

But a stop meant more time to work myself up into a nervous wreck. My face must have indicated as much, because Tomás spoke as if I had protested out loud.

'Natalie, he's never been there!'

I wouldn't have cared, really, I was happy for them and their sparks that were flying around me, but I am a rip-the-Band-Aid-off-quickly kind of girl and this would take forever. I tried to think of it from their point of view: Northampton isn't just any cute town. It's the LGBTQ capital of the Northeast, a place that promised acceptance and solidarity and something for Tomás and Albert to bond over. Unless I was willing to get into a whole conversation about my heterosexual privilege, I would need to just smile and acquiesce. Besides, we would probably be hungry by then.

When we arrived at Miss Florence, my anxiety seemed to melt as quickly as the cubes of butter on my scrumptious blueberry pancakes. I don't know if it was the quaint town, the good company, or just that hopeful feeling that seems to ride along on a road trip, but I was thinking less about the possibility of a disastrous outcome and more about just enjoying the ride. In true buttinski form, Tomás convinced us that we should go all out to surprise Jeremy. Going all out for Tomás always began with the right outfit. Now that I was enjoying myself I was totally game. His plan included a stop at a ski shop in Bennington, where I would buy head-to-toe skiwear so I could disguise myself on set.

I thought for sure Albert would veto the whole thing, but he was so smitten with Tomás that he didn't want to dampen his spirit. I was all in — it was the most fun I'd had since Turks and Caicos. But once I zipped up my ski suit my nerves kicked back in and I begged Albert to call Jeremy and feel him out. What if he never wanted to see me again? Albert dismissed me, saying he didn't want to bother him during filming — a pretty absurd answer, considering we were driving up to crash his set. But I let it go.

According to my close friend and personal concierge, Siri, we would arrive at the set just before dark. This was apparently of great significance, because Albert became particularly adamant that we not interrupt the last hour of daylight at the shoot in any way. We swore we wouldn't, arrived on the set, and did just as we'd promised. I even wore my ski mask to ensure that Jeremy wouldn't recognize me and blow his scene. Albert ran off to pee and Tomás and I stood quietly on the side as discreetly as possible. We were both nervous and excited. It was in between shots and the director was calling for the extras to come up. A group of ski bunnies paraded right by us, and Tomás nudged me into the line. Swept away in the moment, I didn't protest — the right outfit can really give a girl confidence, I guess!

A stylist quickly perused the group, tucking, zipping, and unzipping seemingly at random. When she got to me, she ripped off my face mask. 'Where did this come from?' she asked.

'Quiet on the set!' someone shouted, saving me from answering.

I remembered the scene well from reading the script. Spoiler alert: it was the final scene, an après-ski in front of the lodge, following that frustrating ten to twenty minutes in the last act of a romantic comedy when the boy and girl break up due to some unavoidable obstacle, only to realize the foolishness of their ways and travel by foot/cab/horse, or in this case snowmobile, to reach each other and confess their undying love. The irony was not lost on me.

Jeremy was supposed to sit with his feet up, gazing at the mountain, melancholy, while sipping a hot chocolate. I looked around for him but only saw Albert wildly gesturing for me to cease and desist. I searched the crowd for Tomás, hoping for a nod of support, but he was nowhere in sight. He had been eyeing the craft services cart when we walked in; hunger or nerves must have gotten the best of him. Some ride-or-die chick he turned out to be!

Jeremy walked onto the set in all his glory and my heart dropped to my knees, which both began to wobble. All the confidence that I'd had around him when he was gay seemed to have disappeared, along with any anger I'd felt over the whole misunderstanding.

The director yelled, 'Action!' The scene began just as I remembered from the script. Jeremy sat, sipped, and gazed up at the mountain, the sound of a ski patrol rescue snowmobile revving in the distance. Another skier, fresh from the slopes, ran to him and grabbed him by the jacket. It was Lance Ludwig the Third, Jeremy's character's arch-nemesis.

'It's Nancy — she took a horrible fall,' he said, sobbing. 'I'm not sure she's gonna make it.'

Jeremy stood and shouted with guttural anguish up the mountain, 'Nancy!'

As his cry echoed in the woods, he grabbed his ski poles and headed for her. He was so convincing and I was so crazy for him that my gut impulse was to stop him from reaching her. It was a legit knee-jerk reaction — I stuck out my leg and tripped Jeremy Madison mid-ski, causing him to lunge forward and bang his head on a tree stump. As he grabbed his head and rolled to his side, groaning, I ran to him and kneeled down, taking his face in my hands. He opened his eyes and smiled at me, and I responded by kissing him sweetly on the lips. He stood up and shook the whole thing off like a tackled linebacker at the Super Bowl. He grabbed my arm and raised it in the air like we were champs, and then pulled me toward him for the kiss of all kisses, the one formerly destined for his leading lady.

The director screamed, 'We're wasting light here!' while Albert ordered everyone with a camera to take photos and post them to their feeds. We were trending by sunset.

And so it was that I finally ended up on the pages of the *New York Post*. 'Who is that mystery girl with Jeremy Madison? The enchanting' — that's a quote — 'Natalie Canaris.'

Go on, ask me if Flip Roberts saw it.

My answer? 'I don't know and I don't care!'

31

A. This Story Ends Badly
B. You Won't Feel So Bad About It

By Ruthie, Third Floor, Ladies' Dresses

There are three different types of salespeople in a department store: those who hang out in the dressing rooms ('Do you need another size?' 'We have that in a beautiful aquamarine if you'd like'), those who hang out by the register and get the 'Did anyone help you with this?' leftovers, and those who walk the floor asking if anyone needs assistance. When I first started out I was a big floorwalker, not much interested in gossiping in the dressing room with the other salesgirls.

About a hundred times a day I would say, 'Hi, I'm Ruthie, can I help you with anything?'

The answer was sometimes an enthusiastic yes, but it was usually no. Mostly a polite no, or an 'I'm good, thanks.' But I would sometimes get a grimace or a condescending or impatient 'No, thank you!' I'm sure you've received this kind of 'No, thank you.' The *no* comes with a scowl and the *thank you* comes with a look that says, 'Why are you even speaking to me?' After getting enough of this kind of 'No, thank you,' I stopped asking the question and began walking the floor quietly, just close enough to be of assistance if needed. It was kind of boring. I liked interacting with people and missed the personal contact. But then about ten years ago it got a lot less boring: suddenly everyone and their grandmother had a cell phone. It was then that my decade of eavesdropping began.

The recent obsession with multitasking kicked cell-phone etiquette right out the window of the store onto East 59th Street. What started as a hand-over-mouth, whispered faux pas evolved into a full-volume, I-don't-care-who's-listening conversation. You wouldn't believe the things people feel comfortable yelling into a cell phone in public.

Today I was following a well-dressed woman around the floor as she talked on her cell. It was soon evident that this particular woman was of the horrible variety. She is the center of this story and the reason I began by telling you that A. This story ends badly and B. You won't feel so bad about it.

I won't give her a name, because you know

her and can name her yourself. You met her at summer camp, or in high school, or maybe even just last week at your kid's soccer game. You've spent many a night unable to sleep, going over what you should have said to her in your head, and sometimes you have even woken in a bad mood thinking about her. Her name is _____ _____. We all know her.

She is the friend who greets you with the question 'What are you wearing?' or tells you in the name of honesty that your jokes aren't really funny. The judgmental type who is quick to point out your flaws. 'Overdid it a bit with the tweezers, I see!' she says, laughing as you pull out your compact to examine your eyebrows. It's strange how a compliment can go in and out of our ears in a moment but an insult can fester in there for days, even years.

She was that girl who was part of your fast-formed friend group on your cross-country teen tour, who stopped you at the entrance to the Ferris wheel at the county fair and shook her little finger at you. 'Four per car,' she said. 'Sorry — you're out.' Never to be in again.

She was that girl in tenth grade with the long legs who you were nice to 'cause she was new in town. The one that wrapped those same long legs around the boy you confided in her that you had a crush on.

She was the girl I met my first year in the Bloomingdale's training program. The one who said she'd formed a knitting club: 'Oooh, sorry, Ruthie, I didn't know you knit.' And then, 'Sorry, Ruthie, we all took our boyfriends out for drinks after work and I didn't think you had anyone special so I didn't invite you.'

Or the worst: the one who pretends to be your friend to your face but is the first to talk about you behind your back.

Don't worry — except for the knitting club and the tenth-grade leggy bitch, these didn't *all* happen to me. But I am around women all day long, and I hear a lot of stories. A woman in her late twenties came in just last week for some retail therapy. As she browsed, I could tell she needed an ear to bend; you learn the signs. It was a Tuesday. She confided in me that on Tuesdays she usually met with her baby group. She was one of the founding moms, in fact. But soon some social-climber mom had climbed right over her, winning over all the other moms with nothing but a fistful of her husband's cash. She then changed the group meeting to Wednesdays, knowing it was the only day our girl couldn't make it, on account of her little Johnny having a lazy eye. Wednesdays were when the lazy-eye group meets. Let me tell you, if I ever met that witchy mom myself, I'd sell her a dress that made her look bad from behind!

Stop and think. Who is your nemesis? Even the most popular, confident, put-together adult can call to mind that one girl who made her feel inadequate. *She'll get hers*, you said to yourself, praying that it was true as she walked away from you, leaving you feeling like roadkill to be scraped off the pavement. Well, fill in the blanks, ladies, 'cause today, I promise, she will get hers. Today the road-killer becomes roadkill.

I followed _____ _____ as she weaved in and out of the dress racks, sometimes stopping to feel a fabric, sometimes to look at a price tag. I knew pretty quickly that she was a mean girl of ultimate proportions. Cruella de Vil on steroids. She was on the phone with her friend, asking for fashion advice. Her cruelty was slow and subtle. It began with, 'I need advice because you're my friend,' so that her victim was all eager and ripe for the zinging. Of course I could hear only one side of the conversation, but in my head I heard both. It went like this:

THE ROADKILL: Where are you?
_____ _____: Bergdorf's [she lied].

In the dress department. I want to wear something new to Celeste's birthday dinner. What are you wearing?

ROADKILL: Celeste's dinner? I wasn't invited . . . Do you think it's an oversight? I thought we were close!

_____ _____: Oh, I'm so sorry I brought it up — I just assumed . . . Well, I can call her and ask if you want.

ROADKILL: No, don't. That's so awkward.

_____ _____: I'll just hint at it. I have to ask her something anyway. Call you right back.

Click.

_____ _____ turned to me, holding the Max Hammer dress. 'Do you have this in a small. I don't see a small.'

She was one of those entitled women who assumes that everyone exists only to serve her, so she didn't bother phrasing her demand as a question.

'I'm sorry,' I said, not sorry at all. 'It's the hottest dress of the season — we only have the two larges left. Try one on.'

'I don't have time to try one on and I'm not a large!' she ranted. 'You would think if it's the hottest dress you would have more!'

I hated her. 'I don't do the buying, but I

have been told the manufacturer ran out as well. Sorry, seems you're out of luck.'

When I turned to walk away, she mumbled under her breath, 'Out of luck . . . something you're used to, no doubt.'

Tomás overheard her and stuck out his tongue behind her back. She went back to dialing her phone.

'Celeste! Are you ready for your party? Guess who I just spoke to — Veronica Block! I had no idea she wasn't invited.' She waited a beat. 'Well, you must have forgotten.' She laughed. 'She's easily forgettable!' Another beat. 'Oh, no, I'm sure she doesn't care — she even said she had better plans that night.' And another. 'Yes, I think she said *better*. Maybe it was *more exciting* — can't remember exactly. In any case, you know Veronica and her husband are such bores. What makes a party is who you don't invite, not who you do.' And with that last bit of nastiness she hung up.

She was the worst, this broad. She might take the nastiest-customer-ever cake. But I knew how to get my own quiet revenge on people like her. That sweet, desperate young girl with the long story had returned the overloaned size small Max Hammer this morning as promised. It was even more of a mess than when she left with it, but I didn't

269

care. I went in the back and got it for the nastiest customer ever, hoping that when she got it home and saw what a wreck it was she would try to return it. I couldn't wait to accuse her of damaging it and refuse to take it back. 'I guess you're out of luck again,' I would say.

Nasty was back on the phone again, in mid-conversation with poor Veronica. 'Well, I mentioned it, darling, but she didn't bite. She explained that it's really just an intimate get-together for her nearest and dearest. Maybe next time, you know, when she widens the net.' Poor roadkill Veronica, in way over her head. 'No, I had no idea — a kidney, *really*, well, thank god she didn't need it. You know you should be more careful whom you offer a kidney to, Veronica, really.'

I didn't trust myself not to wring her neck with it, so I gave the dress to Tomás and went out for a smoke. Normally I wouldn't do that to him, but I was still a bit pissed that he and Natalie had left the floor uncovered the other day to go on their little love quest. The last thing I heard was, 'I guess she needed your younger eye to find a small.' I hate to admit it, but that stung. After Lillian I was probably the oldest salesgirl here. Salesgirl — even the name made me feel old. Maybe I needed a two-cigarette break.

I was standing on the corner with Lillian, a few puffs into ciggy number two, when I saw the nastiest customer ever leave the store. I had just told Lillian the whole story. 'There she is!' I pointed. She was just a stone's throw away. My kingdom for a stone.

Lillian took her in. 'She doesn't look so bad. Look, she's helping that old lady get a cab.'

That didn't sound right. I took a look for myself. It was bizarre. She was actually helping an old lady get a cab. She smiled at her and said something we couldn't hear. We craned our necks to try. The old woman thanked her as she stepped into the street and raised her hand for a taxi. The old woman seemed touched by her kindness. And then it happened. A cab pulled over, and the nastiest customer ever became the nastiest New Yorker ever. She got in, slammed the door, and rode away.

Lillian yelled, 'Oh my god, she stole that woman's cab!'

We both rushed to the old lady's aid.

'Did you see what that bitch just did?' she asked as we approached.

I love that about New Yorkers, frail old ladies giving it out like gangsters. As I stepped to the curb to hail her another cab, the ground shook. At first I panicked, thinking it was a bomb. People were screaming as the earth rumbled again. I looked across 59th Street just in time to see the ground open up, like something out of a sci-fi movie, and swallow up the Yellow Cab with everyone and everything in it. I was never one to believe in karma, but on that day I was converted.

★ ★ ★

The next day Tomás and Natalie gathered round while I read them the front page of the *New York Post*. They were both still kissing up to me, trying to make up for their little disappearing act. I was over it — it was nice to see them both so happy. Neither of them had been very lucky with love since I'd known them. I've worked with a lot of younger people over the years, and I can honestly say these two were my favorites. They even invited me to join them on their upcoming double date. I declined, but how sweet are they to have asked?

Natalie thought the headline 'Holy Sink-hole!' was a bit tacky, since a woman had actually died, but the *New York Post* has its own moral compass. From its most infamous headline, 'Headless Body in Topless Bar,' to my personal favorite, 'Osama bin Wankin',' which ran when they found porn in bin

Laden's foxhole, they clearly go for the laugh above all else. I get it — I often have a tendency to do the same. This was as close as I had ever been to front-page news.

The earth really outdid itself yesterday when a sinkhole opened up and swallowed a Yellow Cab, killing one. Onlookers outside Bloomingdale's feared a bomb as the ground shook at the corner of 59th and Lexington. But the culprit was a 10-foot long, 12-foot-deep sinkhole caused by a break in the sewer line. Employees of local businesses say they had noticed a growing crack in the pavement but hadn't thought it anything serious.

The taxi driver, who emergency workers said had been protected by the front cage, survived with a couple of broken bones. Police have yet to release the name of the deceased passenger. She had a Bloomingdale's bag with her, and witnesses confirm that she had just come from the department store.

'Do you think Celeste canceled her dinner party?' Tomás asked coyly.

'Now there's a spot at the table for the other one!' I answered, laughing to myself. I had been calling the wrong girl roadkill!

I knew we sounded insensitive, but really, the woman had been so horrible. I almost felt worse that our beautiful Max Hammer dress had met such a dreadful fate.

32

The Balcony of the Paris Theatre

By John Westmont, Caroline's Husband

I was sitting at my desk in my study looking out the window at Central Park. It's a two-sided desk with chairs on both sides, one facing the interior of the room and the other facing the window. I choose where I want to sit depending on whether I want to concentrate or daydream. I had a tall stack of papers to grade and should have been concentrating on them, but my mind was elsewhere.

I was thinking about Andie, wondering what she was up to and why she hadn't stuck around for that coffee after class last week. My hope was that she had stood me up because she was a good person and knew that although nothing inappropriate was going on, it still wasn't right. A part of me had been relieved. I hadn't felt this way about anyone since meeting Caroline. I wondered if it was just a byproduct of the growing distance between us — if that void allowed for

275

something, or in this case someone, to step in and fill it. It *is* the classic excuse people give for cheating: filling a void.

I knew my marriage felt shaky, but it seemed to me that the problem could be traced to a time before I met Andie. The day-to-day looked the same. Caroline greeted me when I got home with the same warm smile, but now it seemed oddly forced. I asked her many times if something was wrong, but she always denied it. But I felt alone even when I wasn't. There's nothing as sad as feeling lonely when you're lying next to the person who is meant to complete you. Still, I would never use that as an excuse for infidelity. I don't believe there's any excuse. I decided that tonight I would sit Caroline down and insist that we go talk to someone.

Eventually I gave up grading papers and looked up what was playing at the Paris movie theater. It had been weeks since my last visit; I imagined the movie would have changed by now. It had, so I left and hailed a cab to my number-one place to escape.

As I climbed the steps to the balcony, my favorite place to sit at the Paris, my anxiety began to melt away. I sat down in my usual seat, balanced my popcorn on the ledge, and took off my coat. Then I saw her. My heart skipped a beat. Andie was seated at the other end of my row. I felt guilty and exhilarated at the same time. I felt alive. I felt terrified. I felt like I should run. Then she saw me. A smile washed over her face, and I could swear her eyes welled up. The lights went dark and we both silently met at the seats in the middle of our row. We didn't say a word. When the movie began I offered her some of my popcorn. A few minutes later we reached into the bucket at the same time. As our hands touched, the bucket fell to the floor. I grasped her hand in mine and didn't let go for the rest of the film. I can't even tell you if the film was any good, because all I could feel was her hand in mine. When the film ended I felt as if I had been holding my breath. I didn't know what had come over me; I knew this was wrong, but it also felt so natural, so comfortable, so *right*.

As the credits rolled we put on our coats and left the theater, still not speaking. I took her hand again as we went down the stairs from the balcony. At the bottom of the stairwell the light of day shone into the lobby, an unwelcome beam of reality. We dropped each other's hands. I shot her a forlorn smile. She returned the same.

Outside on 59th Street we stood at that particularly Old World cross-section of New

York, looking out at the square in front of the Plaza Hotel.

As a professor of film, I often had scenes from movies running through my head. But this particular location seemed ironic to me now. As Andie bent down to tie her shoe, the final shots of *The Way We Were*, a film about two people who couldn't be together, played before my eyes. Barbra Streisand saying, 'Your girl is lovely, Hubbell,' before running her hand through Robert Redford's hair for the last time. 'See you, Katie,' he says, pain in his eyes. 'See you,' she says to no one as he runs off to a waiting cab.

I had really lost it — a few meetings with this woman who was a virtual stranger to me and I was comparing us to the characters in one of the greatest cinematic love stories of all time. I had to start watching more sci-fi and apocalypse movies. I had a loving family that meant the world to me, and I to them. When Andie stood back up I would say it: 'See you, Andie.' And I would leave. In fact I would run, and never look back.

'Oh my god,' she said as she stood. Her face was white. She looked as if she'd just witnessed a murder.

I touched her shoulder. 'What is it?'

She recoiled. 'Don't touch me!'

I was totally confused. She sighed, looked

again at her shoes, and then explained. She was calm and straightforward.

'John, there is a photographer taking pictures of us from across the plaza. He was hired by your wife, who's trying to prove that you're cheating.'

I couldn't believe my ears. It felt like I'd been sucker-punched. 'How do you know that?' I managed to stammer.

'I know because I'm a private investigator and I sometimes use that same photographer.'

At this point I thought she must be joking. I even laughed, relieved that she was just fooling around. But she went on.

'Your wife, Caroline, hired me a few months ago to try and find evidence that you were having an affair so she could take advantage of the infidelity clause in your prenup.'

'My prenup? What the hell do you know about my prenup?' I was feeling unsteady on my feet. Betrayed. Confused. My heart was racing; my neck felt like it was on fire.

'I told you, your wife hired me as a private eye. I'm sorry, John, but it turned out she was the one having an affair. She's cheating on you but wanted to make it look the other way around, for the money.'

The fountain in the middle of the square

started to spin before my eyes. It was hard to comprehend what she was saying. I steadied myself against the wall.

'Give me a minute,' I said. She lowered her head and let me stand, leaning against the side of a building, while I tried to wrap my head around what was happening here. Was this the end of my marriage?

When I could feel my feet on the ground again, I asked her, 'You mean this was all a setup? You and me — we're a setup to catch me being unfaithful?'

Tears started to run down her face. I felt a flash of anger that she was playing the victim.

'No, no, no!' she shouted. 'Only our first meeting, the one in the dress department at Bloomingdale's — I was on the job then. But I fired Caroline when I found out the truth about her. I guess she's hired someone else. I'm sorry, John, I should have told you, but it's unethical. God, listen to me talking about ethics.'

I looked into her eyes searchingly.

'We never met because of fate. I kept on tracking you even after I fired her. I know that sounds so stalkerish and awful. But the awful thing is, today was truly an accidental meeting.' She paused and looked down, dejected. 'And now, I'm sure, it's our last meeting . . . of any kind.'

I was so nonreactive that she just kept on talking. It was a lot to take in, and I wasn't sure what I wanted to say.

'John, I don't want to contribute to her false case against you. As of now there isn't one compromising photo of us — we came out of the theater like two friends who just saw a movie. If I need to, I will testify to the truth — that she's trying to set you up and that there's nothing going on between us.'

'The photographer is still watching us?' I asked, finding my voice.

She looked over my shoulder. 'Yes, his lens is pointed right at us.'

'Why did you keep tracking me?' I asked her, praying for the words I wanted to hear. 'After you fired my wife — Caroline, I mean — why did you keep following me?'

'I'm sorry,' she said quietly. 'I . . . like you. I missed you. I tried, but I couldn't stay away from you.'

And there it was. All of a sudden the whole mess seemed to resolve into clarity. My wife of twelve years wanted to get away from me so badly that she had resorted to entrapment, and Andie couldn't stay away from me. My silence must have scared her, because her next words were spoken in a tone that was all business.

'Listen to me,' she said. 'This will be a long

fight and most definitely a court battle, but no matter what happens to my career, I will testify about what I've done and what we haven't. I can testify to her attempt at collusion and procurement. It won't be easy, but she will leave your marriage with nothing more than she came in with.'

Scenes from every divorce movie from *Kramer vs. Kramer* to *The War of the Roses* ran through my head. The fountain in front of the Plaza began to spin again. I squeezed my eyes tight. Maybe it was the cinematic setting, maybe it was the sudden moment of clarity, but I knew what I had to do.

In one of the most storied spots in all Manhattan, I took Andie Rand's face in my hands and kissed her with a passion I had not felt in years. In my head I imagined I could hear the shutter of the photographer's camera.

She broke away in protest. 'What are you doing? Are you crazy?'

I smiled at her, feeling sure of myself for the first time in a long time. 'Kiss the girl or waste months in a drawn-out court battle with my cheating wife and, let's not forget, the mother of my child? I am most definitely not crazy.'

I kissed her again. This time she gave in. When we finally came up for air, she laughed.

'That kiss is going to cost you.'

I laughed as well. 'What's five million dollars, give or take, when you have more money than you could ever use?'

She smiled. 'I meant lunch.'

'How about the Oyster Bar?' I asked.

'It's a date.' She laughed again.

'Our first,' I said, taking her hand in mine as we both practically skipped down Fifth Avenue, our own personal photographer in tow. I knew I had a lot of important decisions ahead of me, but for now I would just concentrate on the first: lobster bisque or clam chowder?

33

'Til Death Do Us Part

By Seth Carson, Five-Time Loser
(Soon to Be Six)
Age: Old enough to know better

I work at the Frank E. Campbell Funeral Chapel on Madison Avenue. It might sound to you like I'm saying that with pride. I'm not. The only thing I'm proud of is my biceps. Other people who work here definitely do it with pride. Even the security guard who works the night shift acts like he's guarding the crown jewels. I will say, if you die in New York City, the Frank E. Campbell funeral home is the place to go — the last club worth becoming a member of. You would be counted along with famous actors, singers, politicians, and a whole slew of over-the-top rich people. My boss still goes on about Judy Garland's and John Lennon's funerals, but if I was going to name-drop, I would mention Biggie Smalls and the mobster Frank Costello. I wouldn't have minded being here for those two. Most days are just normal people — normal dead people, that is.

Today I was hoping to be out by five so I could pick up a present for my new girlfriend's birthday, but the undertaking business is so damn unpredictable. That's what my boss was always preaching: *You have to be available, Seth.* 'People don't phone us on Tuesday saying, 'We'll be pulling the plug on Aunt Becky on Thursday.' No one forwards an advance copy of his suicide note to the mortician — 'Feeling desperately depressed and will not be able to hold on much longer. Please expect me next Thursday by three.''

He thinks he's being funny, and everyone makes it worse by laughing at him. Personally, I don't think it's funny at all. Everything else has to be booked in advance — dinner reservations, back waxing, car detailing, everything but death. And that's how the woman from the front page of today's *Post* has jammed up my Friday night.

They brought her in at two to be embalmed. Embalming usually takes around three hours, dressing and casketing around one. My job was just the last part, to dress and casket the body. I wasn't trained to be an embalmer, and I've been told I'm not nice enough to handle the intake process — dealing with grieving family members takes some kind of sensitivity that I apparently don't have. I'm better with dead people. Whatever. I'd been here longer than at any other job I'd had since failing college, and I was getting used to it. Though believe me, it took some getting used to.

I even told my new girlfriend the truth about what I did. I'd lied to the last two girls I got with. But this one seemed so open and understanding. I met her online two months ago. My profile still says penny stock trader, which was actually four careers ago. I haven't held down a job long enough to bother changing it. And this isn't really a job you want to write on a dating profile. But I told her, and she was pretty nice about it. She knew that Heath Ledger had been embalmed here and even thought that undertaking was an admirable profession. Maybe next week I'll tell her that I'm not really five-foot-nine.

I tried to skip out during the embalming process, but my boss caught me and asked me to assist. One of our top embalmers had cut his hours and it was a scheduling nightmare. My boss was always pushing me to go get my embalming license, saying he would even pay for it if I signed a long contract with him. But there's no way I was ever going back to school. This really was a *dead*-end job.

I told the embalmer, a really strange guy

named Gus, that I was in a big rush. I had to shower and pick up a gift for my girlfriend's birthday tonight. He said he would help me dress and casket too. This was good, except it meant that I had to listen to his endless stories. By the time we were ready for my part it was after five. If I hurried, I would still have time to pick up something for my girlfriend but not to shower. I guess that's what Drakkar Noir is for.

I made the mistake of commenting on the dead lady's casket outfit as I pulled it out of the Bloomingdale's bag. It was a new black designer dress with the tags still on. 'What a waste of a new dress,' I said. This led to Gus rattling off death fashion trivia — an endless list of who wore what to the grave.

'Princess Diana was also buried in a black dress that she had recently purchased,' he said, sounding like a walking, talking Wikipedia page.

I nodded and tried to keep us moving.

'Whitney Houston was buried in so much jewelry that she still needs a bodyguard!' He waited for me to laugh. I didn't.

Just as he started in on whether or not Michael Jackson was buried with his white sequined glove, my boss interrupted, holding a pair of black pumps and an emerald-green suit.

'The family dropped off her clothes . . . Great Scott, what are you two doing?'

'His name is Seth, sir,' Gus answered, like an idiot.

'Two morons,' my boss said, shaking his head.

I wasn't being put in a category with Gus. I defended myself. 'Someone already dropped her clothes off, right there in that Bloomingdale's bag.'

'I told you, that bag was one of her personal effects at time of death. The whole city knows this woman died with a bag from Bloomie's.' He held up the suit. 'This is what the family is expecting.' He put it down and left, still shaking his head and mumbling curses under his breath. I, on the other hand, spent the next hour cursing out loud so everyone could hear except the dead lady in the wrong dress.

34

'Tis the Season

By Ruthie, Third Floor, Ladies' Dresses

The store was extra-bustling, even for the week before Christmas. Probably on account of the view of the giant sinkhole in the ground out the west-side windows. We hadn't been this much of a tourist attraction since the 1970s, when some marketing genius made Bloomie's ladies' undies a must-have NYC souvenir. Today it was so crowded I didn't see Arthur Winters walk quite purposefully through the dress department, but Tomás certainly did. He nearly crawled inside a rack of dresses. We hadn't seen Arthur since Tomás pulled the switcheroo with the dress, and we had no idea how it had all turned out. Obviously Tomás feared the worst. I rushed over to help iron out anything that might need ironing out. Tomás reluctantly followed behind me.

'Hi, Arthur, how are you?' I greeted him, a little too upbeat.

'Very well, Ruthie, thank you. I'm not

being disloyal, but I came to see this fellow — Tomás, right?' Tomás barely nodded his head while diverting his eyes to all available exits. Arthur added, 'My fiancée sent me.'

His fiancée? I met Tomás's eyes, and we both assumed the same thing — he was talking about Sherri. We silently commiserated with each other as Arthur continued.

'She said that you had the best fashion sense of anyone she's ever seen and was hoping that Ruthie would let you slip away to the men's department to help me pick out a suit for my wedding.'

But this had to be Felicia! I remembered that Tomás had spent hours styling her for their first date. I was so happy. Tomás was bursting with enthusiasm. He grabbed Arthur's shoulders and practically shook him.

'You're marrying Felicia? You're marrying Felicia?' he shouted, losing all semblance of professional composure.

Arthur nodded and we both hugged him. He looked utterly confused, and Tomás explained. 'The mix-up with the packages was kind of my fault, and, well, let's just say I've been a bit worried about it ever since.'

'That mix-up with the packages was the best thing that's happened to me in quite a long time.' Arthur smiled.

'It wasn't really a mix-up! We're your fairy

godmothers!' Tomás exclaimed. 'Tell us everything . . . please!'

Arthur explained how dinner at the Four Seasons that night had begun awkwardly but had left him wanting to see Felicia again. And how they had their first kiss in front of the City Hall entrance to the Brooklyn Bridge and now would be going back to City Hall this week to marry.

'Wow, that was quick!' I was so thrilled I could barely contain myself.

'Quick?' Tomás fired back. 'Felicia has been waiting for years!'

Arthur laughed, his eyes glistening with happiness. 'Can I borrow him for an hour?'

'Of course!' I beamed. 'As long as you let me help pick out her gift for your first anniversary.'

'Who else?' He smiled, adding, 'And for my new assistant's birthday as well.'

Score one for middle-aged ladies everywhere, I thought as the two went off to find the perfect suit.

35

Curtain Call One

By Luke Siegel, M.D.
Of marrying age

As I ducked out of Exam One my phone buzzed again. It was getting harder and harder to ignore. The text messages were all variations on the same theme. *Lucas, call me when you have a break. Call me between rounds. Call your bubbe back already, it's not nice.*

Oh, how I rue the day I taught my grandmother how to text. I thought it would be easier than the constant phone calls, but it was worse — even more constant. She had the tenacity of a seventeen-year-old girl looking for an AWOL boyfriend on prom night. I knew what she wanted. Tomorrow night was my Grandpa Morris's retirement dinner. He's been a garment center pattern-maker for seventy-five years. Seventy-five years: a big achievement — record-breaking, I believe. Of course my brother and I were going. But my brother was going with his wife and child, while I barely left the ER long enough for a date, let alone procreation. Becoming a doctor had once cemented my standing as star grandchild, but my M.D. was wearing out its luster with my grandmother. I was nearing thirty, and suddenly the lack of a Mrs. by my side rendered the initials by my name practically inconsequential. My lack of a wife, or even a girlfriend, or even a prospect of either, was the eternal thorn in my bubbe's side, and reversing this travesty, as she referred to it, was the main purpose of her existence.

'I can't die till my Lucas settles down,' she'd say.

To which I'd always respond, 'If that's the case, I never will!'

She would shake her head and declare in Yiddish, '*Nor a shteyn zol zayn aleyn.*' Translation: Only a stone should be alone. It didn't make any sense to me in either language.

I entered Exam Two for my next patient. A restless young woman and her gum-chewing friend both sat, fully clothed, on the table. I reached out my hand.

'Hi. I'm Dr. Siegel. What and who is the problem?'

The gum-chewer answered for her friend. 'We were out celebrating her birthday, and suddenly she couldn't stop itching.'

Sure enough, the other girl was scratching everywhere she could reach.

'Okay. Put on this gown, open in the front, bra and underwear stay on. I'll come back in a few minutes. Do you want your friend to stay for the exam?'

'Yes, please — she's reading me *Entertainment Weekly* to distract me.'

I ducked outside the curtain and texted my grandmother. *What's up, Bubbe?* I typed as the gumchewing friend continued reading: 'Engagements. Maybe you'll be engaged by your next birthday! Seth got you such a nice gift for this one, and you've only been together a short time.'

'Don't get carried away,' the patient replied. 'I mean, it's an awesome gift, but notice who's sitting in the ER with me?'

'Good point,' the gum-chewer answered, and continued. 'Engagements. Actor Jeremy Madison to wed Bloomingdale's employee Natalie Canaras. The two got engaged on the R train in Queens after a flash mob he hired performed 'Your Love Is Lifting Me Higher.' Onlookers said he got down on one knee and proposed with a five-carat cushion-cut ring.'

'Are you ready?' I called through the curtain.

'She's good,' the friend answered.

'I swear I think I'd rather have this original Max Hammer than a five-carat ring!' the itchy girl said as I entered the room.

'Ha, I thought I recognized your dress,' I butted in. I couldn't help it. 'My grandfather works for Max Hammer. Well, he did. He's actually retiring tomorrow.'

'Wow, that's my favorite designer. I'm getting my master's in design at Parsons. My boyfriend bought me a dress of his for my birthday tonight,' she said as she pointed to it, neatly hanging on a hanger like a prize. 'It's, like, *the* dress of the season,' she gushed, momentarily forgetting her itchy agony.

I examined her. Her horrible rash looked like it was roughly in the pattern of the dress.

'I'm sorry to tell you this, but I'm afraid you won't be wearing that dress again. You have contact dermatitis. There are two kinds, irritant and allergic.' I grabbed her chart as my phone buzzed. I took it out of my pocket just to make sure it wasn't an emergency. It read, *Are you bringing a date to Grandpa's party?*

I groaned. They noticed. The gum-chewer came right out and asked, 'What's the matter?'

I laughed. 'Nothing. It's just my grandma — she's driving me crazy with texts.'

The itchy girl, who I couldn't help but notice was quite pretty, thought this was the cutest thing she'd ever heard. I know this because she said, 'That's the cutest thing I ever heard! A grandma who texts!'

'I taught her,' I responded, knowing damn well that *that* would now be the cutest thing she'd ever heard. I was right.

'Oh my god, you taught her, that is the cutest thing I ever heard!' She smiled through her itchiness. She was a trouper. I looked at the chart.

'So, Samantha Schwartz' — Jewish, I noted to myself, silently cursing my grandmother for brainwashing me — 'it says here no allergies. Is that correct?'

'That's right. Well, never before today,' she added sadly. I could tell that she loved that dress.

'Let's get you on an IV of Benadryl, then see what this dress is made of.'

The friend held it up. It *was* the dress of the season. Which I knew only because my bubbe had texted me a picture of it on the cover of *Women's Wear Daily* a few months back with the caption, 'Grandpa's going out on top.' I'm usually not this chatty with my patients, especially given the fact that the pretty one obviously had a serious boyfriend, but my grandpa is my idol, and with his retirement imminent I was feeling extra-proud of him and his accomplishments. I took out my phone and found

296

the picture while the nurse set up her IV.

'Look, your dress was on the cover of *Women's Wear Daily!*' The itchy Jewish girl — Samantha Schwartz — took my phone. She smiled and handed it to the gum-chewer, who looked duly impressed.

'It's her dream to be in *WWD*,' she said.

The Benadryl was delivered and I attached it myself. 'This may make you sleepy, but the rash should start clearing up quickly. Now let me take a closer look at this dress.' As I grabbed the dress, a familiar smell hit me. A deeper sniff of the fabric instantly transported me back to my first year of medical school, when we first began working with cadavers. Formaldehyde — not a smell one easily forgets.

'Where did your boyfriend buy this dress?' I asked.

'Bloomingdale's . . . I mean, it came in a Bloomingdale's bag,' she responded tentatively.

I sniffed it again, in a few different spots. 'I hate to tell you this, but this dress is covered in formaldehyde.'

Samantha Schwartz immediately threw up at my feet and then began to sob loudly. There was absolutely no consoling her. Her gum-chewing friend explained what Samantha's boyfriend did for a living and therefore what must have happened. I have to admit, I almost cried for her. What kind of idiot would take a dress off a corpse and give it to his girlfriend? I've seen a lot of crazy in this ER, but this may have been the worst.

My phone buzzed once again, and this time I welcomed the distraction. Even if it was my bubbe again.

Luke, If you don't have a date I know a nice girl, Mrs. Mandelbaum's niece, who you can bring to the party. I'm worried for you to come alone.

'Is that your bubbe again?' Samantha asked between sobs. She could clearly use some distraction as well, so I told her everything. I smiled. 'She's trying to convince me to bring a date to my grandfather's retirement party. She says she's worried about me coming alone.'

The gum-chewer spoke up. 'She should be worried. So should you. A nice Jewish doctor going alone to a party that's probably packed with nosy grandparents of single girls. You'll be live bait.'

Samantha blew her nose and agreed. 'She's right. Just bring someone — anyone.'

I looked down at her leg. 'Look, the rash is clearing up already.'

She smiled. 'Thanks ... I feel much better.'

'You can get dressed and go ... '

We all realized my blunder at the same time: she had nothing to wear but the death dress. I bit my lip. The gum-chewer rolled her eyes, and Samantha started to sob again.

'Believe me, this isn't the first time an ER patient has had to go home in doctor's scrubs. I'll get you a pair.'

As I left I heard her tell her friend, 'As close as I'll ever get to a Max Hammer. And on my birthday. I want to die!'

Should I? I debated with myself. It wasn't like me, but it *was* the obvious move here. I took out my phone to text my grandmother back.

If I bring a date, Bubbe, do you think Grandpa can get me a dress?

36

Curtain Call Two

By Sally Ann Fennely,
Runway Model /New Yorker /Broadway Star

I waited in the wings just like I had before my first fashion show, only a few months ago. Back then I was scared to walk; now I was scared to speak. I heard my cue and stepped out onto the stage of the Brooks Atkinson Theatre. I felt my breath being pushed out of my body. My first line was coming, and I was sure I would manage nothing more than a whisper. But as I spoke something completely different happened. I became my character. I became Daphne Beauregard.

I was her, fighting for my sanity, fighting my horrible husband, fighting not to be sent away for the lobotomy that I knew was coming. When I cut myself with the pieces of the broken Niagara Falls snow globe during the second act, the gasps from the audience were audible. They were there with me. With Daphne, I should say. All except the three women sitting in the house seats in the third row. My mama, my sister, Carly, and my grandma at their very first Broadway play.

They were there with *me*.

Women's Wear Daily, claiming to have discovered me, wrote a story on it. The writer shared it with me that very night at a little celebration thrown in my honor at Sardi's.

In a rag (trade)-to-riches story, Alabama native Sally Ann Fennely went from the runway to the Great White Way after just a few months in New York. After debuting in the pages of *Women's Wear Daily*, Miss Fennely caught *That Southern Play* producer Earnest Cooper's ear with her beautiful southern accent at Sardi's last month. He brought her in for a reading, and the first-time actress snagged the lead. It is said that Cooper was angry and fed up with Hollywood divas on Broadway after Jordana Winston left the show without cause or warning. He is quoted as saying, 'Why cast a star when you can create one?' He is delighted to have discovered what he feels is a true southern delicacy, Sally Ann Fennely. From the rousing applause and the buzz in the theater following her debut, it's safe to say the audience and critics were delighted as well. Ms. Winston, who is in Japan shooting a diet soda commercial, could not be reached for comment.

37

Finale

By Luke Siegel, M.D.

I picked up Samantha Schwartz the next night, brand-new Max Hammer dress in hand. She changed into it and came out looking absolutely stunning. It was an odd thing to be surrounded by your whole family on a first date. I was especially dreading the introductions. I mean, what did I really know about her except that she had lousy taste in men? The generic 'How did you two meet?' was bound to come up, and I wasn't sure how I would answer. But the night was so filled with toasts and dancing and wonderful stories about my grandfather that no one really paid us enough attention to pry. And the pretty girl by my side was like kryptonite to all the meddling yentas in the room.

My grandfather's young associates spoke of everything he had taught them and the honor it had been to work so closely with him. They vowed they had learned more from him than any single professor at RISD or Parsons or

FIT. Samantha was clearly in awe. They spoke of the Yiddish words they'd picked up, and some even worked a few Yiddish expressions into their toasts. One said his biggest compliment at work to date had been when my grandfather had called him a mensch. One woman talked about my grandfather's sense of humor, his endless teasing and witty observations about their generation. With tears of love in her eyes, she told of how he had happily learned to text, but when emojis became popular he was really up in arms. She imitated his Polish accent: 'It took me so many years to master the English language, and you are right back to communicating with hieroglyphics like cavemen!'

There were seven or eight speeches. The room was filled with the celebratory sounds of laughter and cheers, tears of happiness, and applause. But the room fell silent when Andrew, Max Hammer's son, asked my grandfather to say a few words.

Morris Siegel, my grandfather, told the story of being saved by happenstance by Max Hammer himself at the age of thirteen on a boat to America. He spoke about their early years in this country and the importance of making a life that counted enough for all those they had left behind. By the time he was through there wasn't a dry eye in the house. Being a doctor can sometimes make you feel like your job is so important, with people's lives hanging in the balance, depending on you. But my grandfather's life and his explanation of what it meant to him to make dresses for women humbled me.

'For seventy-five years I have made ladies' dresses. That means that for seventy-five years I have made women happy. For seventy-five years I have made mature women spin around in front of the mirror like young girls. For seventy-five years I have made young girls look in the mirror and for the first time see a woman staring back at them. I have made young men's eyes pop out. I have made old men's eyes pop out. Because the right dress does that. It makes an ordinary woman feel extraordinary. And like my Mathilda, all women are truly extraordinary. It's just not often that they get to wrap themselves up in a bow and show the world.

'On the occasions that they do, the dress is everything. No one receives an invitation to dinner or a wedding or a ball and says, 'Oh, I need to buy a new hat.' They say, 'I need to buy a new dress.' No one spends weeks searching for the perfect sweater or blouse, but the search for the perfect dress can lead a woman to visit every store in the city. It's the dress that needs the right bag, the right shoes, and the right shade of lipstick, never vice versa. The dress a girl wears to a prom, on her first trip down the aisle, even on her second, is probably the biggest decision of the night. In fact a bride may spend more time contemplating the dress than the actual proposal. I can promise you it wasn't those ill-fitting glass slippers that gave Cinderella the confidence to crash that ball. It was the dress — the dress made her do it!

'I am a modest man, but if I'm not going to say it now, when will I? I am proud that I have made thousands of women feel beautiful. That my creations have turned heads and warmed hearts. I am proud that Max Hammer dresses hang in closets wrapped in memories of all the special occasions when they were worn. Unlike me, a beautiful dress knows no age. It is boundless. A beautiful dress holds a little bit of magic in it. A dressmaker like myself is lucky to be the magician. I am grateful to have known all of you, grateful to have known Max Hammer, and grateful to have spent my life decorating the lives of extraordinary women.'

★ ★ ★

Somewhere in the middle of the speech Samantha put her arm through mine, and we stood together, listening. I felt an unexpected connection to her. I caught my grandmother looking back at us more than once, and it almost made me want to let go of Samantha. But I gave in to the warmth of the night and let my bubbe really have it all. Besides, I liked the way Samantha's arm felt in mine. I'd never been one to bring a girl home to my meddling family. But it felt nice to be sharing the moment so intimately with someone else — someone there just for me.

I wondered to myself if a dress could really hold so much power. I looked at my pretty date in her Max Hammer dress, tears glistening in her eyes, and wondered if what my grandfather said was true. As if reading my mind, he came over and gave me a big kiss on the cheek. He took Samantha's hand in his and spun her around. 'Magic,' he said.

She did look quite beautiful. But magic? I wondered.

'How did you two meet?' he asked.

I felt nervous. Samantha noticed and responded for me. 'We met because of one of your little black dresses,' she said.

She was right. We had. Maybe it was magic after all.

Acknowledgments

I owe a debt of gratitude to many people, some of whom I mention below.

First and foremost, to my editor, Claudia Herr: It has been a complete joy to go through this process with you. Thank you for being spectacular and brilliant and extraordinarily patient.

To Valerie Cates, for championing my story and having such confidence in it and in me.

A HUGE thank you to my fierce and fabulous agent, Alexandra Machinist, and to everyone involved at ICM.

To my UK editor, Selina Walker: thank you for sharing your ingenious insights.

To Judy Jacoby, Suzanne Herz, Todd Doughty, and Victoria Chow at Doubleday for loving my book, spreading that love, and showing me the ropes.

To Sophie Baker at Curtis Brown for corralling all of the foreign affection for our little American black dress.

To Mara Canner for never saying no and to George Sheanshang for always saying yes.

To Linda Coppola, Andrea Levenbaum, Ellen Crown, and Phoebe Kline: I wrote a lot of words before these words. Thank you for reading and encouraging nearly all of them and for your pivotal help with this project.

For my entire life I have been surrounded by a loving family and true friends whom I treasure. You are my anchors. Thank you for embracing my crazy and my writing.

To my mother, Florence Levenbaum: I have no words to aptly describe the love and encouragement you have given to me throughout my life. You inspire me and I love you very much. Thank you.

To my three beautiful, passionate, and supportive daughters: Raechel, Melodie, and Talia. Separately, each of you is remarkable; together, you are unstoppable. I should only live up to the spark of love for me I see in your eyes. You inspire me every day to be a better woman, mother, and person.

A little extra gratitude goes out to my youngest daughter, who fought a brave battle while I wrote this book. Talia Ruth Rosen, reader number one: your strength, courage, and discipline amazed me daily and kept me moving forward. You are my hero.

And finally to Warren, my husband and my very best friend. They say to write what you know, and if I know anything at all I know true love, and that is because of you. To quote Bruce Springsteen, our poet laureate:

'Through the wind, through the rain,
the snow the wind, the rain
You've got, you've got my, my love
heart and soul'

We do hope that you have enjoyed reading this large print book.

Did you know that all of our titles are available for purchase?

We publish a wide range of high quality large print books including:
Romances, Mysteries, Classics
General Fiction
Non Fiction and Westerns

Special interest titles available in large print are:
The Little Oxford Dictionary
Music Book
Song Book
Hymn Book
Service Book

Also available from us courtesy of Oxford University Press:
Young Readers' Dictionary
(large print edition)
Young Readers' Thesaurus
(large print edition)

For further information or a free brochure, please contact us at:
Ulverscroft Large Print Books Ltd.,
The Green, Bradgate Road, Anstey,
Leicester, LE7 7FU, England.
Tel: (00 44) 0116 236 4325
Fax: (00 44) 0116 234 0205

Other titles published by Ulverscroft:

EMMA'S PLACE

Noelene Jenkinson

Thirty-something jeweller Emma Hamilton returns to her childhood hometown of Tingara, a charming historic village in the foothills of the Australian Alps. Builder Malcolm Webster commutes to Tingara from nearby Bendigo each weekend to work on restoring a beautiful old Victorian homestead. When the two meet, attraction flares — but Mal is young; and Emma, wary after her failed marriage, is not in the market for romance. Will Mal's humour and charm break down her barriers?

THE PRIDE OF THE MORNING

Pamela Kavanagh

1850s England: Emma Trigg has always accepted her grandfather's wish for a union between herself and her cousin Hamilton. Their marriage will ensure a continuation of the equestrian tack-making business on Saddler's Row, satisfy her aunt, and provide Emma with a secure future. But at Chester's Midsummer Fair, a chance encounter with personable horse dealer Josh Brookfield sparks a whole different chain of events. A friendship is severed, long-held secrets come to light, and Emma is drawn down an uncertain path. Can she ever forget the man with laughter in his eyes and the soul of a poet?

MOORLAND MIST

Gwen Kirkwood

Emma Greig has seen little of the world when she leaves school at fourteen to become a maid at Bonnybrae Farm, a life far removed from her carefree schooldays. The Sinclair family both welcomes and rejects her: Maggie is kind and warm; her brothers, Jim and William, playful. But the haughty Mrs Sinclair, disturbed by her children's friendship with a maid, resolves to remind Emma of her place in the world. When Emma and William defy her and strike up a closer bond, Emma is sent away — and William banished from the farm he loves . . .